Key West

The Companion Episodes

Inspired by real events

By Peter Wick

From the Author:

As always I would like to thank Robert Silk. In addition I would also like to thank Tim O'Hara, who gave us an informal guided tour of historical landmarks of Key West, and reminded us often that he should be charging us.

There was a moment in April, 2013 when Robert Silk and myself discovered the real Papy's mausoleum locked. To Robert I would like to say it is probably better that you were not able to get in and leave a copy of the novel with the coffin.

Key West Episode One – One-way Ticket was first published as a Kindle-only novella by Wheelman Press in October, 2013. Key West Episode Two – Cooking The Books was also published by Wheelman Press as a kindle-only novella in October, 2013. Key West Episode Three – Papy on Trial was first published by Wheelman Press as a Kindle-only novella in April, 2014.

Key West – The Companion Episodes, Azzurri Publishing edition
©2015 by Peter Wick

Cover design by Ross Denyer

__Politician:__ __n.__ An eel in the fundamental mud upon which the superstructure of organized society is reared. When he wriggles he mistakes the agitation of his tail for the trembling of the edifice. As compared with the statesman, he suffers the disadvantage of being alive.
-Ambrose Bierce

Contents

Episode Three:
Papy on Trial

Episode One:
One-way Ticket

1
The Briefcase

The briefcase was gray, like the cloudy Washington, D.C. sky.

Davis closed the door to the taxi, and tossed a few bills through the front window at the driver.

He carried the briefcase up the stone steps, past the gold-plated letters that said, "Federal Bureau of Investigation," and through the revolving doors.

Who could say what was in the briefcase? Who could say there ever was such a briefcase? Even the taxi driver could not remember it.

2
VANISHED

By the time the story broke Davis was back in Tallahassee, Florida, conferring with Bernie Papy on their strategy moving forward. That would be Florida State Representative Bernie Papy, King Of The Keys to several of his colleagues. To the FBI he had been convict number B527, until he was freed on bail…Assuming he actually paid bail.

Papy was officially out on bail, but rumors were swirling; was any bail actually paid? Was it "Bail," or was it another pay-off?

The vote-buying charges, leveled against him by other state representatives, had not gone away, but to watch Papy work, you would never know he was under any scrutiny whatsoever. You would never know that he was facing an upcoming trial for an ever-growing list of illegal activities and operations.

Perhaps he knew what others were just learning, that the primary witness against him, former Key West Police Chief Darrel Martins, would not pose as big a threat as once thought.

When the news reached the offices of The Miami Herald, it felt to everyone involved like a punch directly in the gut.

Key West Police Chief Darrell Martins, witness to Papy's corruption, participant in Papy's corruption, convert, turncoat, rat, now a protected federal witness, was gone.

Gone.

That's all anyone knew.

Vanished. Like a puff of smoke in the breeze.

It was 1951 now. Barely, but there it was. The calendar had opened on another year of Papy's corrupt control of Key West.

Trumbull and Murphy walked soberly into Miami Herald Editor Lee Hills' office. Trumbull closed the door behind them. The three men eyed each other silently for a moment.

"He's just gone?" Hills asked.

"That's right," Trumbull said. "My source says it has to be an inside job.

"No Martins…" Hills trailed off. "How much of a case do they have without him?"

"That," said Trumbull, "is exactly the point."

Hills eyed Trumbull. "We have to be careful," he said. "If Papy has bought his way that deep into the FBI, we can only print information we can prove."

"Papy thinks he has us beat," Trumbull said. "Our job is to prove him wrong."

"So how do you propose we go about this?"

Murphy, who had been silent up to now, cleared his throat suspiciously. Hills and Trumbull turned.

"Murphy," Trumbull said, "what's going on in that head of yours?"

"Look, Trumbull," Murphy said, "don't take this the wrong way."

Hills turned from Murphy to Trumbull, smiling. "Easy, Trumbull. Let's hear him out."

Trumbull did not respond. He looked at Murphy.

Murphy cleared his throat again and continued. "Everybody knows who you are. Nobody knows who I am. Okay, a few people do. My point is, I can poke around a little without drawing as much attention as you."

"Murphy," Hills said, "Are you asking to take the lead on this?"

"All I'm saying is, Trumbull walks into someone's office and…it's Trumbull! It's his 'Dear Cuz' column. It's, it's muck-raking at its most potent, but it's also a train engine coming down the track. You hear Trumbull coming. You get my point? I walk in and maybe they don't put up a big brick wall right away."

A pregnant silence sat among the three men.

Hills looked from one to the other. He smiled.

Trumbull looked down at the floor, contemplatively.

Murphy could not stand the silence. "What I'm saying is –"

"You're right," Trumbull said.

Murphy stood motionless. He was in disbelief.

"You're gonna have a helluva job, Murphy," said Trumbull. "You'll have to smooth-talk your way into the confidence of some pretty scared people. FBI agents, people who know the people who know. Scared to talk, scared to be seen talking. Hell, I don't want to do that anyway; pussy-footing around, treating scared people with kid gloves. Do what you got to do."

Murphy was slightly stunned by what he had just heard.

Hills sat up in his chair and began collecting things from the top of his desk.

"Well," Hills said. "You two don't need my input. I guess I'm just the editor around here. No one bothers asking me anything anymore. You just decide what you're going to do on your own."

"What's got into you?" Trumbull asked.

"And don't even bother telling me what you're going to do, Trumbull," Hills said sarcastically. "I don't even want to know what you have up your sleeve."

"What's the schedule?" Trumbull asked. "How long till Papy's trial?"

"Two months," Murphy said.

"And the censure vote," Hills added. "That's sooner. Next week, I think."

"The censure vote," Trumbull mused. "Do you really think the state legislature is going to censure Papy?"

"It's a distinct possibility," said Hills.

"Murphy, let's meet back here next week after they vote on the censure. Let's show this clown we mean business."

Trumbull went to the door and out.

Murphy stood facing Hills.

"Where's he going?" asked Murphy.

"Where do you think?"

"Key West?

"That's my guess."

"But the story's the FBI," Murphy said. "Washington…Tallahassee."

"And Key West," Hills said.

"How?"

"Don't know yet, do we?"

Murphy thought for a moment. Finally he said, "I'll need an expense account in Washington."

"See Betsy. She'll set you up."

Murphy nodded with relief.

"And don't get too excited," Hills said. "There's a reason Trumbull didn't want this."

"What's the reason?"

"You ever try gathering information out of anyone in Washington?"

"Not yet."

"Well…" Hills trailed off. "Just remember, you don't get to complain. You wanted it."

Murphy nodded. He stood where he was, unsure if the meeting was over.

Finally Hills looked back up at him. "You still here?"

Murphy took a breath. "I'll uh, I'll see you in a week," he said, and closed the door behind him as he left.

3
I Want To Retire Well

Judge Nathan McCarthur was a large round man. The desk in his private chamber was also large, but he dominated the desk, both in size and composure.

His private chamber had two entrances. The main one led to the courtroom. The smaller one led to a labyrinth of hallways. Only Judge McCarthur and a few select colleagues knew their way through the maze of hallways.

McCarthur sat at his desk reading a brief, and absently dipping a spoon into a bowl of soup.

There was a knock at the door to his right – the smaller entrance.

"Yes," McCarthur yelled.

The door opened and Davis walked in. McCarthur looked up from his papers, soup spoon half out of is mouth. He peered over the top of his reading glasses.

"Hi Davis," he said. "Been wondering if you were going to pay me the pleasure of a visit."

"Your Honor," Davis said respectfully, as he moved to a large chair facing McCarthur's desk.

"Well." The judge carefully placed the spoon back in the soup bowl. He set the brief down on his desk and gave Davis his full attention.

"Papy says hello," Davis said. "He wanted you to have this." Davis pulled a bottle of wine from inside his coat and handed it to the judge.

McCarthur took the bottle. He rotated it and peered at the label. McCarthur's eyes widened.

"Very nice," McCarthur said. "Rare vintage."

"Have you looked at the brief for Papy's case?" Davis asked, motioning toward the stack of papers on McCarthur's desk.

"I have," McCarthur said. "Good read. Has a lot of plot twists."

11

"Have you given much thought to how it ends?"

"Davis, let's get one thing straight," said McCarthur. "I don't like your boss, Bernie Papy. I think it would be poetic justice, after everything he's done, if he went down for putting a damn bill in some milk-toasts palm in the state assembly building. I mean, that's what we're actually trying him for, right? Giving this, what's his name, Traynor, a hundred dollar bill? It's a joke. It's like Capone going down for tax evasion."

"Careful, Your Honor," Davis said soberly, "You're in danger of passing judgment before the trial begins."

"I'm not passing any kind of judgment. I'm sitting here having a bowl of soup, chatting informally with you. Passing judgment is what I do when I'm wearing a robe."

"Papy will be speaking to the legislature, Thursday," said Davis.

"Fine. Great. He's speaking to the legislature. Davis, that's neither here nor there. The legislature censuring or not censuring Papy means nothing to this case."

"You Honor," Davis said, shifting forward in his seat, "this is all a horrible misunderstanding. This trial is a sham."

"Not yet, it isn't," McCarthur said. "But you'd better hope it becomes one. Judging from the mysterious disappearance of the FBI's star witness, this uh, this uh Police Chief, Martins, it would seem maybe we are headed in that direction."

Davis was quiet for a moment, looking at the judge contemplatively.

"Dismiss the case," Davis said.

The judge did not respond right away. He picked up the bottle of wine and read the label again. "This is nice wine, Davis," he said. "I know Papy paid well for it." He set the bottle down and looked at Davis. "The case will move forward. Papy will have to make things look a lot better than they do right now."

"Meaning what?" Davis asked.

"I want to retire well," the judge said. "Next year. Papy is guilty. We both know that, sure as the nose on your face. Now I don't know what happened with this vanishing police chief. I don't want to know. What I'm saying is, Papy has to win in court, or at least appear to win in court. It has to look good."

The faintest trace of a smile played across Davis's mouth. He stood up.

"Thanks for your time, Your Honor," he said.

"And don't draw attention to yourself," said McCarthur. "The last thing I need is some damn reporter letting everyone know you visited me."

4
Back in Town

Dear Cuz;

Sometimes there is a difference between what you know and what you can prove.

Papy lives somewhere in the dark corners of that difference.

I might know that Papy is as rotten as a week-old fish carcass, but if I can't prove it, Papy wins.

So there are some things I know that I cannot say.

I would just like Papy to know that, from where I sit, the stench of rotten fish is wafting wind-ward. The fish carcass smells old, putrid, and no amount of cash, no backroom deals, no strong-arm tactics, can make a rotten fish smell sweet.

It stinks.

So far I cannot say exactly where the rotten fish smell is coming from, but I intend to sniff it out.

-Trumbull

Trumbull was used to this drive now; Miami to Key West. It had been a few months, but it felt like a comfortable familiar drive.

He was feeling at home during the final few miles. Every turn in the road, the familiar house just before the sharp left turn, and then the pothole in the middle of the lane.

Finally he pulled up to the hotel. The concierge smiled as he approached. His usual room was available.

He unpacked, set the typewriter on the desk, and looked out the window.

He watched the people on the street going about their lives. He looked a few blocks further and saw crusty old fishermen docking their boats after a long day at sea. On the dock others were gathering nets, telling stories the way only crusty old fishermen can tell stories.

Trumbull could stare out the window at fishermen anytime. Tonight he had something else to do.

Ten minutes later he was outside walking down Duval Street.

He felt a chill as he neared the familiar sign of the Boat Bar. He walked inside and felt comfortable among the familiar noisy clatter.

He walked past the roulette wheel where, as usual, someone had just lost a small fortune to the house.

He approached the bar. He leaned on his elbow as the bartender turned to him. The bartender did not recognize him at first.

"Scotch on the rocks," Trumbull said.

The light went on inside the bartender's head. He smiled at Trumbull.

"I should know your name," said Trumbull.

The bartender turned to him with his drink. "My friends call me Teddy."

"Well, Teddy, good to see you again."

"What brings you back?" Teddy asked.

"Does something have to bring me back? Maybe I've just grown to love Key West."

"I doubt that," Teddy said.

"Where're my old friends? " Trumbull asked. "Walter, Tweedle Dum, Tweedle Dee?"

"They'll be in," said Teddy. "Walter anyway. One of the two guys ain't around no more."

"No? There's just one of them?"

"Long story," said Teddy.

"Well, my job is writing stories," Trumbull said. "You'll definitely have to fill me in on that one."

"I forgot, you're trouble. Remind me not to talk to you."

Trumbull detected a smile on Teddy's face as he turned to fill a customer's drink. Then, as Trumbull turned to the door, Eva walked in.

Eva was exactly what Trumbull would have wanted, if he wanted anyone. She was a woman, not a girl. She had the lines on her face that most women fear, but some women make classic. She was strong. She feared nothing. Almost nothing, anyway.

She ran the local 'house of ill repute.'

And now… Eva and Trumbull had a history.

Their eyes met. Eva looked surprised. She walked across the room toward Trumbull.

She smiled at Trumbull as she approached. He didn't smile back. He didn't show any emotion at all.

"Hi," she said simply, sitting on the bar stool next to him.

"I wasn't sure if you were still around," Trumbull said

She paused before responding. "Yes," she said. "I'm still around."

"Are you in business?" he asked.

"I have a new place set up. Not as good as the old one, but a girl's got to keep busy."

"Have you been contacted about testifying?" Trumbull asked.

"Testifying – "

"The trial, Papy's. It's two months away. I'm sure you heard about Martins."

"Do we have to talk about that?"

Trumbull looked at her. He knew she had been compromised in some way. He didn't need to press her for details right away. "What do you want to talk about?" he asked.

"I don't know. Baseball."

"You follow baseball?"

"No. you can teach me all about it."

"I don't want to talk about baseball," Trumbull said.

"Fine," she snapped. "We can just drink and feel awkward."

Trumbull was not amused by her sarcasm. He turned out to the room and took a drink silently.

"Did you miss me?" Eva asked.

Trumbull was silent. He took another drink. He set his glass down on the bar. He realized the question was still hanging. Eva was already upset by his silence.

"Sure," he said.

"You're a bastard, Trumbull."

"Well, you finally agree with every woman who has ever known me."

"Why did I sit down and talk to you?"

"You couldn't resist my charming manner."

Eva stood up. "Are you going to be around?"

"I am," he said. "How can I get in touch with you?"

"Why do you want to get in touch with me?"

"I have some things to talk to you about, some questions."

"Ask me now."

"You didn't want to talk about it now."

Eva looked down at the floor and then back up at Trumbull. "Things get complicated," she said.

Trumbull looked intently at her. "Now I know I have to talk to you," he said.

"I'll think about it."

Eva turned and walked back toward the door. Trumbull watched her walk away. As the door closed behind her, Trumbull turned to find Teddy directly behind him, smiling.

"What are you smiling about?" Trumbull asked.

"Nothing, nothing at all," Teddy said.

5
Friends Got To Look Out For Friends

Florida State Representative Stan Franklin was putting on his coat and hat after a long day.

The door to his office stood open as Bernie Papy walked down the hall toward his office.

"Stan!" Papy said, smiling.

"Hello Bernie," Franklin said, shaking his hand gregariously.

"Got a minute?" Papy asked.

"Been a long day," Franklin said.

"This won't take long. Have a seat."

Representative Franklin looked behind him and reluctantly sat in an arm chair. Papy sat opposite him.

"How are the wife and son?" Papy asked.

"Good. Good."

"How old's your son now, seventeen?"

"Eighteen," Franklin said. "Daniel's going to the University of Florida next year."

"Damn! Time sure does fly."

"It does, indeed."

"Well, go Gators," Papy said.

"Listen, Bernie, it's a hell of a thing going on round here."

"It's going to be fine," Papy said.

"Well now, Bernie, listen, I think of you as a friend. I do. But the speaker's very serious about this."

"How often have you heard of a state legislature actually going through with censuring a representative?"

"Bernie, like I said, I'm on your side, but the speaker –"

"Nah, don't worry about the speaker."

"And then there's all this trial business, the FBI and what not. I don't know how you sleep with all this going on."

Papy scooted forward in his chair and became serious. "Listen, Franklin, this thing is going to work itself out just fine. Especially because I know I can count on your support."

"Speaker's putting a lot of pressure on – "

"I'm going to speak to the assembly," Papy said. "I'm going to throw myself on your mercy. I'm going to be humble and magnanimous."

Papy looked Franklin in the eye. A silent moment froze the room.

Finally he broke the silence by saying, "And then you're going to vote against the censure, and clear my name."

Franklin was quiet. He fidgeted absently with the ring on his finger.

"I don't think I need to remind you," Papy continued, "that your voters might be surprised to learn of another child of yours, that Daniel has a half brother that he doesn't know about. And your wife, I think, will be very surprised."

"Bernie – " Franklin trailed off with a sideways shake of the head.

"You're a friend, Stan. You said so yourself. I'm just looking out for you. You support me on this, there's no telling what good things we can do together for your district."

Franklin turned away from Papy and looked absently at the wall.

Papy stood.

He pulled a cigar from his jacket pocket and laid it on the small table in front of Franklin.

"Friends got to look out for friends," Papy said, giving Franklin a pat on the back. "Glad to hear the family's doing well. I would be proud, too."

Franklin could hardly move after Papy left. He picked up the cigar and rolled it in his fingers.

6
The Note On The Pillow

Murphy's first visit to Washington, D.C. began with grand feelings. It was the nation's capital; too much history to process.

The cab driver drove him past the Washington Monument and then past the Lincoln Memorial. Murphy peered out the cab window at the large statue of the 16th President sitting in his giant chair.

The cab driver pulled up to Murphy's hotel. He helped Murphy with his luggage. Murphy tipped him, thanked him, and he drove away.

Murphy struggled with his luggage until a bellhop appeared.

"Sorry sir. My apologies. Let me help you."

Inside, Murphy approached the concierge.

"Murphy," he said, "from The Miami Herald."

"Yes, there we are," said the concierge, lifting a small card from a tray. "Room 517. Here's your key. Please sign here."

Murphy leaned over the sheet of paper, and signed. "I'm expecting a phone call," he said. "It's very important. From the FBI."

"I will connect you immediately should the call come," the concierge said.

"Thanks."

A pleasant but awkward silence fell on Murphy and the bellhop as they rode the elevator together.

Moments later Murphy was alone in his room.

Nice.

Murphy was not accustomed to being pampered. Like Trumbull, all he asked of life was the basic necessities. Comforts made him laugh a little.

He did like the presence of a mini-bar though.

He poured himself a whiskey and sat on the bed.

The comforter was a bit much, he thought; garish colors blended together to create designer overkill.

He pulled the comforter back to expose the pillow.

Murphy froze for just a moment. A folded piece of paper rested on the pillow. He lifted the piece of paper delicately, as if it were combustible. He unfolded it slowly.

"Can't meet as planned. Things are hot. Look for new instructions at breakfast.

–Tanner."

Tanner was Trumbull's contact at the FBI. They were old war buddies. Trumbull had arranged for them to meet.

Murphy folded the paper and looked back at the pillow.

7

OLD JONAH

Trumbull awoke early the next morning. He wasn't sure who to seek out first. He figured Eva would not be up yet, so after coffee and eggs he walked toward the docks where several fishermen were preparing for a day at sea.

"Morning," he said to three old men preparing their nets.

The fishermen eyed Trumbull carefully before responding.

"Morning," said the one to the left.

"My name's Trumbull."

"Miguel," said the man to the left.

"I'm from Miami," Trumbull said. "I write for a newspaper."

The three men began laughing. Trumbull did not understand why, until Miguel pointed to the one in the middle.

"Jonah, you're gonna be famous. They're gonna write about you in Miami now."

Jonah, the fisherman in the middle, laughed a hearty laugh, showing a few missing teeth.

Jonah's face was made of leather, and his white stubble poked out like needles from a cactus.

"Hell," Jonah said, "write about one-a these here fellas. I don't want that again."

"I'm not here to write about you," Trumbull said.

"No?" asked Jonah. "Alright then. Once is enough."

"Who wrote about you?" Trumbull asked.

"Some local fella," Jonah said. "Wrote fer the paper here in town, and then he went and got hisself killed."

Trumbull eyed Jonah. "Do you mean Bill Lee?"

"Yes, I suppose that sounds 'bout right," Jonah said. "He was a helluva nice guy."

"I knew him," Trumbull said.

The men stood in silence for a moment.

Miguel broke the silence with a cackle and, "Ah hell! He made Jonah out to be God's own fisherman."

22

The three fishermen laughed together.

"Do you gentlemen use your boats for other things?" Trumbull asked.

"Well," said Jonah, "how do you mean exactly?"

"Anyone ever pay you to take your boat out? Maybe transport someone somewhere? Something you're not supposed to talk about?"

"Hell yes!" said Jonah, "but I aint gonna talk about it."

The three fishermen shared another round of cackling laughter.

"Well," Trumbull said, "good luck fishing. I might be interested in going out with you one of these days."

"Alright," Jonah said. "Pleasure to meet you."

8

This Is Not About A Newspaper Story

Murphy awoke to a knock on his hotel room door. He sat up, rubbed the sleep from his eyes, and stood awkwardly.

The knock rapped a second time.

"Coming!" Murphy shouted groggily.

He opened the door to find a room service cart and an over-eager hotel employee. Murphy stepped aside and the employee wheeled the cart into the room.

"I didn't order anything," Murphy said.

"It was ordered for you," the man said. "Have a wonderful day."

He was gone.

Murphy stared at the cart. He lifted a lid. Eggs. Another. Toast.

He shook his head in confusion and reached for the coffee pot. As he lifted it something caught his attention.

A small note had been placed under the coffee pot. He set the pot down and reached for the note.

He unfolded it.

"Tonight: 10pm. Go to the bar, Jimmie's, at 223 Taft. Use the restroom, then go out the back door."

The note was unsigned.

He thought back to the night before, and the note on his pillow. "New instructions at breakfast," that note had said.

Murphy spent the day vacillating between pleasant Washington, D.C. tourism, and worrying about what he was getting himself into. No wonder Trumbull didn't want this, he thought. He wanted to begin calling the FBI, asking around for anyone willing to talk. What can it hurt, he thought. But he held back. He knew he needed to talk to Tanner first.

At 9:30 that evening he stepped into a taxi cab and gave the driver the address for Jimmie's.

Moments later he was inside a bar full of men with loosened ties and even looser lips.

Murphy stepped into the bathroom. On his way out he turned to his left and followed a hallway to a back door. He stepped out into a dark alley. He walked tentatively, unable to see.

He banged into a garbage can, grabbed it nervously, anxious to quiet the clatter.

Then a voice came from the shadows to his right.

"I can't be your source."

Murphy strained to see the outline of a hat and coat in the dark alley.

"Are you Tanner?" Murphy asked.

"Yes. I can't be your source."

"Why not?"

"What did Trumbull tell you about me?"

"You're friends. You helped bring Papy in."

"Now Papy is free on very cheap bail, awaiting trial. Martins is gone. What does that add up to?"

Murphy thought quickly. He wasn't sure what Tanner expected him to say.

"I don't know what it adds up to. That's why I'm here."

"If I'm not your source, are you still prepared to go through with this?"

"Of course," Murphy said.

"I don't think you understand what you're into here."

"What don't I understand?"

"This is not about a newspaper story."

"What's it about then?" Murphy asked.

"Do you have any idea the contempt these men have for you journalists?"

"I have an idea, yes."

"When you think about what has happened, when you think about who these men are, what conclusions do you come to?"

"We don't know what has happened," Murphy said. "That's why we're asking questions."

Tanner exhaled. Murphy's eyes were adjusting to the dark. He could make out the angles of Tanner's face.

"You'll never see Martins again," Tanner said. "No one will. That doesn't just happen. People don't disappear from FBI custody. It was planned at a deep level. But no one will ever know. I won't know."

"I can't accept that," Murphy said. "I have to keep looking."

"There's nothing there. It's pointless to keep looking for something that isn't there."

9
I Love My People Too Much

Representative Traynor, in his customary wire-rimmed glasses and bow tie, stood nervously at the front of the Florida State Assembly Chamber.

"And…and as Representative Papy reached, I thought to shake my hand, to my shock he presented money to me in this hand of his. I dropped the money and left, wondering what sort of man is this? What manner of man has such low principles?"

Papy was near the back of the chamber, standing with representatives Henderson and Franklin.

"What manner of man?" Papy muttered under his breath. "What manner of man are you, kid?"

Only Henderson and Franklin heard him, and they remained fixated on the proceedings.

"Order! The chamber will come to order!" The booming voice came from the front of the room.

"The Chair recognizes Representative Franklin."

At the back of the room Papy put a friendly hand on Franklin's shoulder. Their eyes met as Franklin began his walk to the front of the chamber.

He stood facing the room. An aide placed a glass of water next to him. He raised the glass and took a drink. He cleared his throat.

"I would like to know," Franklin began, "where all this money is."

A faint wave of chuckles echoed through the chamber.

"I've known Bernie Papy for fifteen years. We've co-sponsored bills. We've fought the good fight on behalf of the great state of Florida. Once in a rare while we have disagreed. If Bernie is putting money into people's hands, how come I haven't gotten any of it?"

Once again faint chuckles echoed through the chamber.

"No," Franklin continued, "the only thing I have received from Representative Bernie Papy is friendship. And that is more valuable than money. Thank you."

Franklin stepped away from the podium and walked back through the chamber.

His eyes met Papy's as he approached the back of the room.

Papy reached out and patted him on the shoulder as the two met.

"The Chair will now recognize Representative Christianson."

A middle-aged bald man approached the podium. He looked out at the chamber and pounded his fist.

"Come on men. All of you. This is a joke. Everyone in this chamber knows how crooked Papy is. He's more crooked than a coat hanger, and you're all afraid to cross him. Hell, last month he offered me a case of scotch if I'd switch my vote on his gaming bill. Wake up, for god's sake. Censure Papy."

Christianson stepped down from the podium and returned to his seat in silence.

"The Chair will now recognize Representative Bernie Papy of Monroe County,"

At the back of the room Papy moved forward. He sauntered toward the front of the chamber. When he reached the podium he turned, nodding to a few particular colleagues in the front row.

"Thank you," he said quietly. "Thank you for giving me this opportunity to address these allegations."

He paused and exhaled.

"Now...I can see where my love for the people of Florida, and my commitment to doing what is right for them, might have, at times caused me to act in a way that could be misunderstood and misconstrued. I can see, in looking back, that maybe I do love representing my people a little bit too much. But can you fault a man for loving his constituents? Can you pass judgment on a man who only wants what is best for the great people of Florida?

"Now, as to the claims that I have offered things, money, to some of you, this has all been so terribly misunderstood. I apologize if my generous and caring nature sometimes appears to have strings attached.

"There are no strings attached. I love to give. Giving is healthy. The good book tells us it is better to give than to receive. Now, Representative Christianson, did I once offer you a case of some of the best scotch available in these parts? Indeed, and I want you to have it still. It is a gift. There are no strings attached.

"Gentlemen, I am at your mercy. I humbly apologize if my actions have ever had the appearance of wrong doing. You do what you feel is right. I am innocent of these charges, but I trust your judgment. I will honor your decision. Thank you."

Papy walked slowly down the aisle between the assembly seats. He smiled at several of the representatives as he passed them. He smiled at Traynor, who quickly diverted his eyes.

10
Your Biggest Mistake Yet

Eva heard the knock on the door and stood up from her chair. She was surprised to find Trumbull standing in the hallway.

Without saying anything she left the door standing open and walked back to her chair.

"Well," Trumbull said, "you didn't shut the door in my face. I'll take that as a good sign."

He entered and closed the door behind him. He tossed his hat and coat on the bed.

"Sorry about the other night. It's good to see you again."

"What're you doing here?"

"I came to see you."

"As a reporter?"

"As me. I am who I am, Eva."

Eva looked up at him inquisitively. "I have to ask this question one more time; did you miss me?"

"Yes," Trumbull said. "I missed you, Eva. They don't make 'em like you anymore. There's no other dames in this world who have what you have."

Eva thought for a moment. Slowly she smiled. She stood up and looked directly at Trumbull. "You know, coming back here might have been your biggest mistake yet."

"How do you figure?"

"What's the downfall of every man?" she asked. "What's his Achilles heel? The weak point? The chink in the armor?"

"A woman," Trumbull said.

"You're after Papy. You want to know what happened to Martins, and here you are with me. I'll lead you astray. I'm your weakness."

"No, you're going to help me."

"I'm not as strong as you, Trumbull."

"You're stronger than any woman I've ever known."

30

Eva put her hand on Trumbull's cheek. Then she turned and walked away from him. "What do you want to know?" she asked.

"Whatever you got. Whatever you've heard."

"I don't know anything for sure. I just hear rumors, people trying to impress the girls."

"Go on."

"He's buried on some island."

"Martins?"

"Yes," Eva said. "And one of the two guys, you know, who cut you."

For a brief moment Trumbull re-lived the moment, the cold steel entering his abdomen, the fleeting thought that this might be the end, the cold calculation that he would survive, and find his vengeance.

"Why him?" Trumbull asked. "Why the goon?"

"I don't know. I don't – I don't even know if this is true."

"Which island?"

"Who knows?" Eva said. "There's dozens of empty islands out there."

"They had to take a boat," Trumbull said. "Do you think the fishermen know?"

"I'm sure they do," Eva said. "I think it was Old Jonah's boat they took."

"Old Jonah," Trumbull said reflectively.

"You ever hear the story about the man who died climbing to the top of the mountain?" Eva asked.

Trumbull looked suspiciously at her. "No," he said, "haven't heard it."

"Mountain climber, obsessed with reaching the top of the most dangerous mountain. It was all he lived for, just because someone told him when he was a kid that he would never accomplish a damn thing. So finally he climbs the mountain, reaches the top. And a blizzard blows in, and an avalanche kills him. Achieving his goal killed him."

"What's your point?" Trumbull asked.

"This is a messy business you're in," Eva said. "People are disappearing, dying."

Trumbull finally sat down. He was in a chair facing Eva. "It's a good story," he said.

"Don't hate me, Trumbull," she said. "I'm saving my own skin."

"What did they promise you?"

"This," she said, gesturing to the room around her. "Getting back to work, making a little money."

"And in exchange you don't testify?"

"That's right."

"Good," Trumbull said. "Let them think you're squared away."

"I am squared away," she said. "I won't testify."

Trumbull eyed her intently. Finally he broke the gaze and showed a faint smile. "You're talking to me, Eva. I'm going to go out on Jonah's boat tomorrow because of this conversation. You're not squared away. You're just as dangerous to Papy as you ever were."

Eva smiled. "Maybe you're my Achilles heel. You'll be my downfall."

Trumbull stood and walked to her. He reached his hand down and took hers. He pulled her to a standing position. They were inches apart.

He leaned in and kissed her. She reached her arms around his neck and gave in fully to the kiss.

11
Four Went Out. Two Came Back

The next morning broke pleasantly over Key West.

A ray of sun angled in through Eva's window and awoke Trumbull early. He sat on the edge of the bed, trying not to wake her as he dressed.

Soon he was outside, walking toward the docks.

Jonah and Miguel and a few others were preparing their boats with supplies. They noticed Trumbull approaching and slowed their preparations.

"Morning," Trumbull said, tipping his hat back slightly.

"Mornin' it is," said Old Jonah. "It looks like a fine mornin' for fishin'."

"How much would you need to tell me about Martins and the goons?"

Jonah laughed, exposing the gaps of his missing teeth. "I don't need nothin', cuz I don't know what happened."

"You do know," Trumbull said.

"What I know," Jonah responded, "is that they took my boat out without me. Paid me damn well for it too."

"Who? How many?"

"Well," Jonah said, looking off at nothing, "Four of 'em went out. Two came back."

Trumbull thought for a moment. "Four...Martins and the two goons?"

"And that son-of-a-bitch Walter," Jonah said. "He's the one handled the boat. He done it before. Otherwise I wouldn't'a let him near the controls."

"So just Walter and the other one came back?"

"Yep, that guy lost his friend. They're buried out there on one-a them islands, or maybe the sharks et him. Impossible to find, either way."

"Except," Trumbull paused. "Except that two people know where they are."

"Well hell," Jonah squawked, "if you wanna risk askin', it's your funeral. I sure aint gonna bother no one. It didn't happen s'far as I'm concerned."

"Where can I find him, the goon?" Trumbull asked.

"Well, he's gonna be havin' his usual breakfast down at Mabel's, I suppose. He's there 'bout this time every mornin'."

Trumbull pulled some cash out of his pocket and handed Jonah a few bills. "I'm hiring you for the day," Trumbull said. "I'll be back in a few minutes."

"Alright," Jonah said, admiring the bills.

Trumbull walked up the street and turned left. Mabel's was three blocks away. After walking two of the blocks Trumbull could make out the figure of the goon's head from behind. He was sitting at an outdoor table, leaning over a plate of hash browns.

Trumbull walked confidently up behind the goon, and before the goon could react, Trumbull had removed the goon's knife from one side of his belt, and a .38 revolver from the other side.

"Get up," Trumbull said.

The goon stared blankly from his seat.

"I said get up."

He stood awkwardly.

"We're going for a boat ride," Trumbull said.

The goon was silent.

They walked together back down the street and found Jonah inside the boat, warming up the engine.

"Get in," said Trumbull.

The goon stepped up into the boat. Trumbull untied the ropes, tossed them into the boat and stepped over the railing himself. Jonah revved the engine and inched the boat away from the dock.

Trumbull stood over the goon and asked, "Where are we going?"

The goon said nothing.

Trumbull looked at Jonah.

"S'alright," Jonah said. "I have an idea. We'll get close, anyway."

Trumbull looked down at the goon, shaking his head. "You'll talk," he said, and he turned his gaze out to the open expanse of water ahead of them.

12
You're Telling Me But You're Not Telling Me

Murphy had spent two days in Washington, D.C. but had turned up nothing. No one at the FBI had anything to tell him.

He was waiting for word from Tanner about another meeting, but their first meeting had left him so frustrated, he had begun thinking about returning to Florida empty-handed.

Then another mysterious note came, hidden underneath another room service coffee pot.

Later that night Murphy repeated his cab ride to Jimmie's, his casual trip to the bathroom, and his exit out the back door into the dark alley.

He moved slowly, allowing his yes to adjust to the darkness. This time he saw Tanner's silhouette before Tanner spoke.

"What have you found out?" Tanner asked.

"Nothing," Murphy said. "No one's talking."

"Who have you asked?"

"Whoever I can get a phone contact for. Attorney General's Office, a dozen different bosses of yours at the FBI."

"What did the Attorney General's Office say?"

Murphy shook his head. "An investigation is on-going. No comment at this time."

"There's no investigation," Tanner said.

"There's not?"

"They're just waiting for you to lose interest and move on to the next story."

"There's no investigation. Are you telling me this? Is this on the record?"

"No," Tanner said in a hushed worried tone. "I'm not telling you this. I'm not telling you this as a reporter. I'm telling you as a person, for your own safety. Lose interest in this story."

Murphy thought quickly. He was not sure what to do. "Why are you telling me this? Why not just let me go home with a strike-out?"

Tanner was silent.

Then it slowly dawned on Murphy what Tanner was doing.

"You're telling me this, but you're not telling me this," Murphy said. "How high up does this go? How could something like this happen? Does it go to the top?"

Tanner remained silent.

Murphy swallowed, processing Tanner's silence.

Tanner finally moved for the first time in several minutes. "You and I never met," he said. "I can't confirm anything. All I can say is, you're very perceptive."

"How do I prove this?" Murphy asked.

Tanner turned and began walking away.

Murphy watched his silhouette recede down the darkened alley.

As Tanner reached the street he ducked into a car and sped away.

13
Oatmeal

Old Jonah had been steering the boat out into open waters for about an hour. He was slowing the boat now.

Trumbull saw islands in the distance, a small collection of islands, rising gently up out of the water.

Jonah cut the engine and the boat drifted quietly.

"Them's the Marquesas," Jonah said.

Trumbull looked down at the goon, who had hardly moved for an hour. "Jonah," he said, "You have a small piece of rope? Something we can tie his hands with?"

Jonah reached past a tackle box, and pulled out a two-foot long piece of rope.

Trumbull took it, and with his foot pushed the goon to his left. He tied the goon's hands behind his back with the rope, and stood over him. "Marquesas," Trumbull said. "Is that where your friend and Martins ended up?"

The man looked up at Trumbull. He puckered his mouth and spat toward Trumbull, but the ball of spit was caught by the wind and sailed harmlessly out to the water.

"Well hell," Jonah said with a laugh. "I don't know 'bout you, Trumbull, but I can wait all day for this horse's ass to talk."

Jonah stepped up to the bow of the boat and held his hands over his eyes, gazing off at the islands.

Trumbull poked at the goon with his foot. The goon kicked back angrily.

"You know, we aint goin' nowhere," Trumbull said. Then he turned to Jonah and shouted, "Jonah, how's the fishing out here?"

"Goddamn!" Jonah said, still standing on the bow of the boat. "Holy goddamn!" He jumped back down into the cabin and stood next to Trumbull, pointing. "We got company."

Trumbull followed Jonah's crooked pointing finger out towards the water. He noticed an odd disturbance at the top of the water about fifty feet away, moving steadily closer to them.

Trumbull realized what it was. "Sharks," he said.

"A whole goddamn family of them," said Jonah.

Within moments they had reached the boat, and were circling it.

"Look at them beautiful god-forsaken creatures," Jonah said. "Specimens, they are. Look at that one."

He was pointing at the largest shark of the group, a fifteen-footer that swam with powerful elegance around the boat.

Trumbull reached down to the goon, grabbed him by the shirt collar, and by his tied hands, and yanked him to his feet. "Look at that," Trumbull said. "Look at that beautiful hungry creature."

The goon did not respond. Trumbull pushed him down to his knees, his head hanging out over the railing of the boat. The shark-infested waters swirled just below. The goon swallowed hard and coughed.

"Yes," Trumbull said. "Look! How would you like to be dinner? What do you think, Jonah? He'd be pretty tasty, huh?"

Jonah laughed again. "Oh sure. He'd go down nice and easy, like a damn sea trout."

Trumbull moved closer to the goon's ear, speaking quietly, directly into it. "So, now is when you open your mouth and tell me what I want to know. Because if you don't start talking in the next 60 seconds, I'm going to toss you in. Don't think I won't. I like these sharks. These hungry sharks are God's beautiful creatures, like Jonah said, and it would be a particular pleasure to feed them with your sorry ass!"

The goon coughed again. His body convulsed. He jerked once, twice, and then released a stomach-full of vomit into the shark infested water.

"Oh, now that's just a cruel joke you're playing on them!" Trumbull said, pulling the goon fully back into the boat. "That's like offering someone a steak and giving them oatmeal."

The goon wiped the spittle of vomit from the corners of his mouth and fell back against the wooden bench, breathing heavily.

"Well," Trumbull said, "What'll it be?"

The goon continued to breathe heavily, his chest rising and falling with each breath. He tried to calm himself. His stomach convulsed once more, but he stopped it before vomiting. He let his head fall backwards and rest against the wooden wall of the boat. "Okay," he said.

Trumbull looked at Jonah, and nodded. He looked back at the goon.

"What was that?" Trumbull asked. "I didn't quite hear you."

"Okay," the goon said. "I'll talk."

Jonah laughed a loud cackle and shook his head.

14
Empty Handed

“No, no, nothing I can write up anyway.”

Murphy was in his Washington, D.C. hotel room speaking on the telephone.

On the other end of the line his editor, Lee Hills, sat at his desk, annoyed.

“Nothing?” Hills asked.

“Nothing. No one will talk. Everyone’s scared.”

“And Trumbull’s contact?”

Murphy sighed. “He’s afraid of losing his job. He knows something, alright, but he won’t go on record.”

“What did he say off the record?”

“Well,” Murphy rubbed his face. “I’ve got to talk to you first about that. And maybe talk to Trumbull too.”

Hills sat forward at his desk. “This was an expensive trip, for you to come back empty-handed.”

“What can I say?”

“Alright,” Hills said, “get on the morning train. Go to Tallahassee.”

“What’s going on?” Murphy asked.

“The state assembly is having their censure vote day after tomorrow. It won’t mean anything one way or the other. A vote to censure won’t have any teeth in it. But if they vote him clear, that’s a story.”

“Yeah,” Murphy agreed. “If they vote him clear, Papy wins a nice victory.”

“And the whole rotten mess just gets messier.”

“Alright,” Murphy said, “I’ll get on the morning train.”

15
Are You For Real?

This time when Eva heard the knock on the door, she knew it was not Trumbull. She didn't like the sound of the knock. She stood and approached the door hesitantly.

"Yes?" she said through the closed door.

"Eva, it's Cranston and Walter. We'd like to talk to you."

Eva opened the door and walked back to her chair.

Cranston was Martins' successor, the new chief of police of Key West. He was shorter and heavier than Martins had been. He seemed to be wedged into his perpetually too-tight uniform. But he was a loyal enforcer of Papy's.

Cranston, along with Walter – wearing his ever-present hat – entered Eva's room and closed the door.

"Special occasion," Eva said. "Both of you at the same time."

Walter sat on the bed and did not say anything. Cranston sat opposite Eva in an arm chair.

"Hello Eva," Cranston said.

"Well," said Eva impatiently, "Get on with it, whatever it is."

Cranston looked toward Walter before responding. "Eva," he said, looking down. "Eva, you know we have eyes and ears everywhere in town. You know that, right?"

"I'll save you some trouble," Eva said. "Yes, Trumbull spent the night with me. What are you going to do about it? Get jealous?"

Cranston again looked toward Walter, who was peering at Eva from under the brim of his hat.

Cranston cleared his throat. "Um, Eva, suppose we set up sort of an agreement before we continue this here conversation."

Eva looked at him with thinly veiled disgust. "What sort of agreement you have in mind?"

"Suppose," Cranston continued, "just suppose that if you were to be, um, uh, forthcoming with us, that uh, that we could see our way clear to maybe finding you one of the premier properties here in town to move your business. You know, a classy joint, where you could reasonably ask for top dollar and feel like you was worth, um, you know, worth top dollar."

"My girls are already worth top dollar, Cranston."

"Why then you want to give them classy digs to, to uh, to ply their trade."

Eva laughed. "Are you for real, Cranston?" she asked sarcastically.

"And I don't think I need to remind you of the, the uh, the consequences of failing to be forthright with us."

"Just what are you guys searching for?" Eva asked. "I don't know anything about anything."

"Now Eva," said Cranston, "I hardly think that's true."

"Well, it is true," she snapped.

"Eva, Walter here is suffering from the mysterious disappearance of his deputy, Mr. Rodriguez. He's gone missing. Hasn't been seen all day."

"Well, Walter I can see you're all broken up. Condolences."

Walter continued to glare toward Eva without changing his expression.

"We have it on, uh, on good authority," Cranston continued, "that Trumbull, after spending the night with you, hired a boat this morning."

"Look," Eva said. "Trumbull left before I woke up this morning. I slept with Trumbull. We fornicated. There, you happy? How the HELL am I going to know what he did after he left? I've been here all day."

Cranston turned back to Walter. He contemplated Eva's answer for a moment.

Walter finally raised his head up. "Eva," he said quietly. "You are walking a very thin line here. Your fate is in your hands. We will come back and discuss things with you again. Between now and then, I would think very carefully about your answers, if I were you."

Walter stood up from the bed and adjusted his hat.

Cranston stood also. "Pleasure talking," he said.

Once again Eva laughed. "Cranston, don't take this the wrong way, but you could learn a thing or two from Walter here about not being a complete dork."

Cranston looked hurt, but tried his best not to show it.

16
Crooked on My Own Terms

"What'cha got there?"

McCarthur turned to his right and watched Davis as he moved from the door to the big chair in front of McCarthur's desk.

"This here," McCarthur said, "Is a brief for a case involving the worst kind of corruption I've seen in some time."

Davis sat and faced McCarthur. "Is that Papy's case?"

"You really need to knock before you come barging in here like that," McCarthur said. "Suppose I had someone high and mighty in here, and you come waltzing in through that door."

Davis cleared his throat, masking any minor embarrassment. "So…" he said, "Have you done any more thinking about what we discussed last time?"

"Have I done any more thinking?" McCarthur sat back in his chair and looked at Davis. "Did you not understand, Davis, that you were the one who was supposed to be doing the thinking?"

"Oh absolutely, and I have. WE have. Word is that the FBI is no longer gung ho to prosecute this case."

"Well, if they withdraw the case, I'll wash my hands of it. But I can guarantee you that ain't going to happen."

"How do you know?"

McCarthur exhaled and set his reading glasses on the desk in front of him. "Let me state it this way, Davis. I am a Judge. I am neither here nor there when it comes to politics. You can't completely buy me off, and neither can anyone else. If I am going to be crooked, I can be crooked on my own terms. The FBI would be embarrassed if they withdraw this case now. Sure, they don't want much more than a token slap on Papy's wrist, but for public relations purposes, they need at least that. Now maybe you and Papy think you've got the FBI taken care of, bought them off, squirreled your way in deep enough to get this star witness to disappear. But what you have to remember is that the FBI answers

45

to more people than you and Papy. I don't want to be the one to break it to you, but your most hated journalist, Mr. Trumbull, is dead right. Papy is amateur hour. This case is moving forward. It'll be a sham, but it's going to happen."

Davis shifted in his chair. "Do you have a number?"

"Like I said, if I want to be crooked, I am going to be crooked on my own terms. You need to present me with a number, and I'll decide if it's sufficient."

17
Marquesas

Jonah pulled on the throttle and the boat gently turned parallel to the dock.

"What goes on out here?" Trumbull asked.

"Navy uses this here as a training area. Nice and out of the way. You shoot somethin' it don't blow up someone's house."

Trumbull jumped from the boat down to the dock and secured the rope to a railing.

"Yep," Jonah said, "this is a nice and convenient island, away from everything, quiet. Got about everything you'd need to bury someone and never be discovered."

"Until now," Trumbull said, looking at the goon. "Jump on down here."

The goon did not move. He stood, hands still tied behind his back, looking at Trumbull with a combination of hatred and fear.

"You should know better than this by now," Trumbull said. "I bet Jonah here would love nothing more than to give you a kick from behind and send your ass falling out here head-first."

Finally defeated, the goon stepped awkwardly over the railing of the boat and jumped down next to Trumbull.

"Alright," Trumbull said. "Now start walking."

The goon dropped his head and sighed. Then he moved to his right and began walking over an embankment.

Trumbull and Jonah followed. They continued walking for several minutes. Then the goon stopped.

Trumbull stepped up next to him and looked down.

"Fresh dirt," Trumbull said. "Both of them. What happened anyway?"

The goon did not answer.

"Well, fine," said Trumbull, "I guess we have time for that story later. Hey, Jonah, got a shovel on the boat? Something our friend here can dig with?"

No!" the goon gasped. "No, I won't do it."

Trumbull and Jonah looked at each other.

"I got a pick ax," Jonah said.

"That's something," said Trumbull. "That's a good start."

Jonah turned and started back toward the dock. Trumbull shouted after him, "Look around your boat. Maybe something else'll work too."

"I'll look," Jonah said.

Trumbull looked back at the goon. He raised his eyebrows and turned to look at the view. A gentle breeze blew across the island. In the distance Trumbull could see another small fishing boat trolling the sea.

"You're crazy," the goon said.

Trumbull turned back toward him. "Hm?"

"You're crazy if you think I'm going to do this."

"Oh you'll do it," said Trumbull calmly.

The goon kicked awkwardly at the dirt in front of him. Trumbull laughed a brief laugh and looked back to see if Jonah was on his way back.

18
Censure

There was an electric buzz in the Florida State Assembly building. The buzz echoed through the hallways.

Inside the chamber the representatives were arriving. They greeted each other in semi-circles around the room, glad-handing, patting each other on the shoulder, smiling and nodding.

Murphy was still tired from the trip, but took his place in the press gallery alongside a host of other journalists.

A reporter from a rival paper recognized him and squeezed between some of the crowd to approach him.

"Murphy," the reporter said.

"Millhouse," Murphy responded.

They shook hands and exchanged pleasantries.

"Trumbull here?" the reporter asked.

"No. It's just me. Trumbull is off doing god-knows-what in Key West."

"What do you think they're going to do here? Will they censure Papy?"

"Who can say? "Murphy responded.

"Helluva thing, huh? Only in Florida."

A gavel rapped loudly from the front of the room, and the chatter quieted slightly. Murphy and Millhouse turned toward the chamber and sat in the uncomfortable chairs behind them.

The buzz of hushed conversation continued around the chamber for few more minutes.

The gavel rapped a second time, followed by, "Order! The chamber will come to order."

The chatter tapered off to a respectful silence, as the gentlemen found their seats.

Murphy searched the room for Papy, as the speaker mechanically read through the formalities. He did not see Papy at

49

his usual seat, nor did he find him near the door of the chamber, where he often chatted and conferred with his colleagues.

Papy was not present.

Murphy crossed his legs and settled in, wondering what it meant.

He wouldn't wonder long. Papy was merely waiting for his moment.

The speaker shouted out the formal instructions, reminded everyone that they were voting to censure their colleague; "Reprentative Bernie Papy, of Monroe County. The clerk will call out names one at a time. Please vote with an 'aye' or 'nay.' And the vote will be so recorded."

Then the grand double door at the back of the chamber swung open and Papy entered the room like a king. The buzz erupted again and the glad-handing, the chatter, the smiles, all as slick as Murphy had ever seen. It caused a tightness in Murphy's stomach.

"Order! Order! The chamber will come to order."

The buzz once again quieted. Papy threw a couple of final hand-waves to colleagues, and then found his seat among the Representatives.

"Representative Crandell."

A brief pregnant moment passed before the first vote was heard.

"Nay!" shouted Representative Crandell from the back of the chamber.

Papy turned and smiled toward Crandell.

"Representative Deloit."

"Nay."

"Representative Duncan."

"Aye!"

A hush came over the room as this first vote against Papy settled on all present.

"Representative Ebbersley."

"Nay."

Murphy turned to Millhouse, and the two shared a knowing nod.

The next morning a thousand young newspaper boys throughout the state of Florida would sing in unison, "Paper! Paper! Papy beats censure vote!"

He had beaten it handily. Those who voted to censure would feel alone and defeated.

Papy felt – once again – vindicated, and he let the world know. He used his favorite phrase to denounce the press; "witch hunt," and he would use it with a particular venom he had not used before.

Murphy, after phoning in his report, had caught the late train to Miami, and slumped into the seat, bone-tired.

He could not sleep, though. It wasn't because of the movement and rattle of the train. He could not sleep because the events of the past week nagged at him. They chewed at him doggedly. He stared out the train window watching the night pass by, lost in a jumble of anger, fatigue, and calculating analysis.

19
Diego Rodriguez Spills The Beans

Dear Cuz;

There has been a lot of buzz about Bernie Papy beating the vote to censure him in the Florida State Assembly.

I expected it. To someone like Papy, controlling votes in the state assembly is just another day at the office. This censure vote meant nothing.

There is also the matter of his upcoming trial. Papy faces charges of buying votes in this very same state assembly. Papy thinks that controlling the fate of the trial is also just another day at the office.

And he would be right, except for the brave confession of one Diego Rodriguez.

I have to apologize to Mr. Rodriguez. I have not been fair to him in the past. When he and his friend Raul cut me, some time ago, and left me bleeding in a Key West alley, I was a little bit upset and began referring to them as "goons." Diego has proven to be so much more than a goon. I want to be sure and spell his name right. He wouldn't want it any other way. "Rodriguez" with a "Z."

Diego Rodriguez felt guilty about helping Papy put the fix into the upcoming trial. You see, Cuz, the FBI's star witness disappeared. Former Key West Police Chief, Darrel Martins, somehow vanished from FBI custody. There was no trace of him.

There was no trace, that is, until our good friend Diego Rodriguez was overcome with guilt and insisted on taking me to the Marquesas Islands, where he had helped bury the deceased Martins in a shallow grave.

Next to Martins grave was that of Diego's friend Raul. Diego was eager to fill me in on this interesting story. It seems that once Martins realized he had been given an all-expenses paid one-way ticket to the Marquesas Islands, he was not exactly happy with the news, and he gave as good as he got. When Raul tried to go at

Martins with his trusty knife – a knife that I am all too familiar with – Martins performed a dazzling trick of defensive combat, and ended Raul's life unceremoniously.

Diego was understandably distraught and in the heat of the moment, put an end to Martins' own life.

I wanted to be sure to mention one other thing. Diego felt strongly that I should also include the name of Walter. Everyone in Key West knows Walter. No one – not even Diego – seems to know Walter's last name, but Diego felt strongly that I should include Walter's name in connection with these tragic events. Diego insisted.

Diego feels terrible about his participation in these tragic happenings, so he understandably insisted on filling me in on everything.

He is worried about how much longer he will live, having exposed these secrets so publicly, so I told him how he can stay completely safe; go on living openly in Papy's Key West, and don't worry about a thing. I pointed out to Diego that in writing this column and running it on the front page of the Herald, I have inoculated Diego against Papy's anger. If anything happens to Diego Rodriguez after this column is published, everyone will know that it is Papy exacting his revenge.

Diego Rodriguez cannot be touched. He has exposed how Papy and his cronies killed Darrel Martins and buried him on a deserted island. Now that we have proof of this crime, should anything happen to Diego Rodriguez we will all know who is responsible.

Bernie Papy is backed into a corner.

I'm curious to see how he tries to wriggle free from this one.
-Trumbull

20

Another Good Bye

Eva sat in the passenger seat of Trumbull's car. The car sat idly at the curb. Trumbull stared blankly out at the quiet street.

"So, good bye again, Trumbull," Eva said.

Trumbull looked over at her. "How'd we get so attached to each other?" he asked.

"How does anyone get attached to anyone? It just happens. It defies all reason."

Trumbull turned his head to the side, thinking. "I live and work in Miami. You run a whorehouse here in Key West. I have to get back."

"I know," Eva said, reflectively. "It never makes any sense."

"Like we said, neither of us is made for relationships."

"Yeah, so we're perfect for each other."

Trumbull looked over at her. "Papy's trial is only going to get closer. Have you thought about what you're going to do?"

"No," she said, "and I don't want to."

"There's a lot going on between now and then," said Trumbull. He looked her in the eye. "I'll be back quite a bit in the coming months."

"To work," she said. "To write."

"And to see you," Trumbull said.

Eva smiled, leaned over and kissed Trumbull on the cheek. She stepped out of the car, and Trumbull started the engine.

Eva stayed on the curb as Trumbull's car eased out into the street and down the block, eventually turning out of sight.

She sighed, then turned around and went back inside.

Episode Two:
Cooking The Books

1
Dollar-deals

Florida State Representative Bernie Papy sat at the head of the table like a king reigning over his fiefdom.

Cigar smoke filled the room. Liquor bottles and glasses littered the table top.

Police Chief Cranston sat at the other end of the table, to Papy's right. Directly across from Papy sat Walter, silent as always, watching, taking it all in. Between Walter and Papy sat Davis, jotting notes on a pad of paper.

Two other men sat to Papy's left.

"Now wait," Cranston said, scrunching his face in a confused twist, "Who owns this land, the county or the state?"

"The state did own it," Papy said, a hint of a smile playing across his lips.

"So the state sold it to the county?"

"Technically, no," Papy said.

"But you said the county owns it now."

"Well," Papy said, smiling more broadly. He leaned back and looked at Davis. Davis put his pen down and turned to Cranston. "We put a little rider on a bill this past session," Davis said.

"A what? A rider?" Cranston's understanding was not becoming any clearer.

"Yes, a rider," Davis said. "It's something you add to a bill before it is voted on."

"So you had a bill about waterfront property here in Key West?"

"No, certainly not," Papy jumped in. "You put riders on bigger bills, State budget, building roads, things that have nothing to do with the rider."

Cranston shifted his overweight body sideways in his chair. He looked from Papy to Davis. "I don't understand none of this so far, but it sounds to me like you're up to your old tricks, Papy."

"I don't think of them as tricks," said Papy, raising his glass to his lips as he spoke. "I prefer to think of them as 'strategy.'"

"Alright," Cranston said, "get on with it. How does the county wind up owning a bunch of property that the state used to own?"

Papy turned to Davis again, and leaned back in his chair.

Once again Davis turned to Cranston. "We put this rider on a bill that, well..." Davis smiled an uncharacteristic smile. "The rider says Monroe County owns the land."

A pleased silence settled on the room.

"You mean you just said it?"

Papy lifted his head victoriously, and said, "We attached it to a bill funding school kids' safety. No one even bothered to read the rider. Passed with overwhelming support. The next day, the school children of Florida enjoyed increased safety in their schools, and..." he trailed off.

"And?" Cranston said.

"And," said a man named Harrison, one of the two sitting to Papy's left, "we are happy to announce that Monroe County is the new owner of several prize pieces of waterfront property on Key West, Stock Island, hell you name it, the best property in all the Keys."

"And," said a Mr. Douglas, the other man sitting with Harrison, "we have right here a freshly minted property deed, spelling out a particularly sweet group of plots, which we hereby sell to our good friend Bernie Papy for the suggested retail price of – "

Papy was laughing. Harrison and Douglas were smiling broadly. Davis tried to remain stoic but was on the brink of failure. Only Walter managed a serious expression.

"What's the price?" Cranston asked.

"One dollar," Douglas barked.

"Sold!" Papy slapped a one-dollar bill on the table and raised his glass.

Miami Herald Editor Lee Hills sat at the head of the large conference room table.

Unlike Papy's table, this one was cluttered with signs of work; papers, pens, take-out food, coffee cups.

To Hills left sat the city editor, the political editor, and two assistant editors. To his right sat Trumbull, Murphy, and two other reporters further down the table.

Hills' feet were up on the edge of the table as he finished reading a page of copy.

"It's good," he said, dropping his feet to the floor. "Drop the part about the fraud allegation. It's unsubstantiated. The rest is damn good reporting."

The city editor took the copy from Hills and scribbled a note in the margin.

"What else?" Hills asked.

A reporter at the far end of the table said, "The D.A. is holding a press conference tomorrow at noon. Suspicion is he's announcing a run for mayor."

"You want it?" Hills asked.

"I know a guy in his office," the reporter said.

"You know a guy?"

"I have a source," the reporter corrected himself.

"Alright, it's yours?" Hills scooted toward the table. "Anything else?"

Everyone looked from one to the other, questioningly.

"Okay," Hills said. "Other business." He looked to his right, cocking his head toward Murphy.

Murphy perked up a bit.

"Murphy," Hills said, "remember that conversation we had a few weeks ago about opening a bureau in Key West?"

"Yes."

Trumbull was suddenly more alert. "It came through?" he asked.

"Approved this morning. We've already sent a couple front office people down to find a space."

Murphy hesitated, then said, "So, that means – I'm – "

"You said you wanted it," Hills said.

"I did. I do," Murphy blurted awkwardly. "How soon?"

"How soon can you go?" Hills asked.

"Soon. Now. As soon as you want me," Murphy said.

Trumbull turned his head half-way toward Murphy and muttered, "Ain't getting any action in Miami. Key West might do you some good."

Murphy playfully elbowed Trumbull in the jaw as chuckles echoed around the table.

Hills leaned forward and cleared his throat. "The Miami Herald Key West Bureau," he said.

"Rolls off the tongue," said Trumbull.

"It's gonna be Papy's most hated phrase," Murphy said.

"Hills-" Trumbull began.

"Don't get too excited, Trumbull," Hills cut him off. "Murphy's the full time guy for a reason. I need hard news reporting."

"But I'm going, too," Trumbull said.

Hills smiled one of his two-part smiles. It was a smile that said he knew Trumbull would do what he wanted no matter what Hills told him. The other part of the smile was appreciation; appreciation for what he knew Trumbull would add, through his "Dear Cuz" column and through his personal history going up against Papy.

"Ah, hell," the city editor said, "Trumbull just wants to make sure Murphy stays away from his girl."

"Jealousy rears its ugly head!"

Cackles and hoots resounded, until all present realized Trumbull was not laughing along with them.

An awkward silence settled on the room.

Trumbull finally raised his head and looked from one colleague to another around the table. "If you're referring to Eva," Trumbull began, "she is not my girl." He paused and glanced at a few of the men in succession. "She's not mine or anyone else's. She is, though, ten times the woman any of you have ever had in bed." He paused again and turned magnanimous. "With all due respect to those with lovely wives."

"Or with not so lovely wives," the city editor blurted, lightening the mood.

The meeting had officially ended, and all present were standing gathering papers into untidy stacks. Shop talk took the place of official business. Trumbull and Murphy stood and turned toward each other.

Trumbull gave Murphy an approving nod and sarcastically muttered, "But I do need you to stay away from her."

Murphy smiled and tucked his papers under his arm.

3
DIEGO

Diego Rodriguez was in hiding.

Ever since Trumbull wrote his "Dear Cuz" column about their little adventure on Old Jonah's boat – explaining how Diego Rodriguez identified the grave of former Police Chief Darrel Martins, as well as that of Diego's former partner-in-crime, Raul – ever since Trumbull spelled out the key role he played, Diego Rodriguez was scared to show his face in public.

Old Jonah let him sleep in the cabin of his boat.

To Jonah it was all entertainment. Old Jonah did not take sides in any of the local arguments. He had been around too long. He wasn't for anyone. He wasn't against anyone. He was entertained by everything. He chartered his boat to whoever paid. He laughed at everyone and respected no one.

He went out fishing and let Diego Rodriguez help. Diego wasn't a bad shipmate. He could handle tackle. He wasn't a bad fisherman himself.

Jonah had warned him, though, that if anyone came looking, he wasn't going to protect Diego.

It was early morning and Jonah was loading his gear onto the boat for a day of fishing. Diego woke up in the cabin with a hangover brought on by a bottle of cheap rum that Jonah was kind enough to buy for him.

Diego was in a foul mood.

"God damn it!" Diego barked as Jonah dropped a box of supplies onto the cabin floor.

Jonah laughed. "You know, when I bought that bottle, I thought maybe it would last a couple of days."

"Shut Up," Diego snarled.

"Well, hell, you can get off the boat if you're gonna be that way."

61

Diego did not say anything for a few minutes. He sat up and rubbed his face, and tried not to feel sick.

Jonah finished loading the boat and started the engine.

"You want to be just a little bit useful?" Jonah asked.

Diego did not respond.

Jonah shook his head and stepped to the stern of the boat, untying a rope and pushing the boat out from the dock.

Jonah stepped back up to the wheel, and guided the boat away from Key West.

Diego Rodriguez felt the subtle motions of the boat as it rocked gently on the morning waves. He held his stomach. He was still trying desperately not to be sick.

Then they passed the wake of an incoming boat, and as the starboard side of the cabin lurched up and then shimmied and then came back down, Diego failed in his attempt to not be sick.

4
Damn Reporters

The papers were signed, the dollar bill pocketed, and everyone raised a glass to Papy's land deal.

"To Papy," Cranston shouted.

"To Papy," the others echoed.

Glasses were tipped back all around, followed by cynical, satisfied smiles.

Alright," Papy said, "on to other business,"

The men around the table quieted down and turned toward Papy.

"Go ahead," Papy said to Davis.

Davis arranged some papers and cleared his throat.

"Diego Rodriguez," Davis said.

Walter raised his head slightly at the end of the table.

"What plan do you have?"

Walter leaned forward. "Do we have to have a plan? Can't we just go when you say go? Let's just take care of him."

As Davis was about to respond, Papy raised a hand to intervene. "We have to plan it," Papy said.

A pause hung over the table.

"Our concern," Davis said, "Is these assholes who write for The Miami Herald."

"They are a pain in the ass, aren't they," muttered Walter.

"We are planning ways to ensure that they do not keep popping up in Key West," Davis said, "but that's a separate issue. In the mean time, everything we do, we do carefully."

"This situation," Papy said, "has gotten out of control."

Papy set his glass down. He was becoming noticeably agitated. "These damn reporters!" he barked. "They don't understand how things work. They don't have any respect for a community that runs things its own way. Goddamn that Trumbull!"

A shiver went through Papy that the others felt.

He slapped his hand on the table and looked out at the men circling the table.

"Who do we have to talk to?" he demanded.

"The dame," Walter said. "Eva."

"Old Jonah," Cranston added.

Papy breathed slightly easier. "I don't think I have to remind you, gentlemen, we are all in this together. This land deal will be very profitable for all of us. We all share in each others' success. Don't cut corners. Be thorough. I'll be here in town for a while. I'm not due back in Tallahassee til the start of the next session three months from now. We have work to do."

Looks were exchanged around the table. Everyone understood.

Papy poured another round of drinks.

5
Carina

Murphy was driving away from the mainland and crossing into Key Largo. Two over-stuffed suitcases sat at odd angles in the back seat. A typewriter without a case angled precariously between the suitcases, and stacks of loose papers filled the nooks and crannies.

By nightfall Murphy pulled up to the small hotel he would call home.

The next morning he turned the key in the lock and opened the door to his new office.

It was modest. Two lonely desks stood facing each other in the middle of a medium-sized room. Someone had planned ahead. The desks were adorned with new typewriters and telephones. A water cooler stood against the far wall.

Murphy turned as a knock tapped at the door.

A woman stood outside. She was young, attractive in a bookish way. Her hair was pulled back. She wore glasses.

"My name's Carina," she said. "Are you Murphy?"

"Yes," he replied.

"I'm supposed to be your secretary."

"I didn't know – I guess I never asked anyone about that. I thought I would be alone here."

"Well," Carina said. "You think maybe I can come in?"

"Oh yes, of course." Murphy was a little bit embarrassed.

Carina entered and surveyed the room. "Hm," she muttered. She turned back to Murphy and said, "Do you want it like this, or can we rearrange a little?"

"Oh, whatever you want to do," Murphy said.

He was struggling not to stammer. As a reporter Murphy had learned to keep his composure in just about every situation. Something about Carina, though, made him feel a little bit weak inside.

"Well," Carina said, pacing around the room, "you'll want me up front, so I can greet people. Can we move this desk over here, facing the door?"

"Whatever you want," Murphy said.

She stood for a moment, looking at him. He felt awkward. She tapped her foot.

"Well?" she said. "You're not going to make me move it by myself, are you?"

"Oh, no, no, of course not."

Murphy moved to the end of the desk and prepared to slide it across the floor.

Carina bent down at the other end. Together they slid the desk. "A little more on your end," she said. "Yes, good."

She stood up straight and put her hands on her hips. "I like it."

"Yes, it's better," said Murphy.

Then, to their mutual surprise, the phone rang.

They looked at each other, puzzled.

"You expecting -?"

"I didn't think it was even hooked up yet."

It rang again. Carina moved as if to answer it, but stopped herself.

On the third ring she reached for the receiver and put it to her ear.

"Uh, um, Miami Herald Key West Bureau," she stammered. "Hm?...Um…hold on a moment."

Carina put her hand over the receiver and looked at Murphy. "He's very angry, whoever he is."

Murphy reached for the receiver. Carina handed it to him.

"Murphy speaking."

The voice on the other end of the line was animated. "Are you the reporter we're going to hang?"

Murphy shifted his feet and glanced toward Carina.

"Well," he said, "if, uh, if you're going to hang a reporter that would probably be me."

"This ain't no joke," the voice on the other end said, and the line went dead.

Murphy held the dead receiver away from his ear.

Carina's eyes widened with the growing realization of what she was getting herself into.

6
First Names

Papy had more than one residence. When the state legislature was in session he stayed at his medium-sized mansion in Tallahassee.

When the legislature was not in session he stayed either at his beach-front house on Long Key, or in his personal top-floor suite in La Casa Bonita Vista, one of Key West's finest hotels.

There was a rumor that he was never charged for the room. In exchange for free residence – so the rumor goes – he prominently displayed the hotel's advertising in the capital building in Tallahassee.

Free room - free advertising. Everyone was happy.

Papy also prided himself in knowing everyone in Key West. He sometimes boasted that he knew every Key West resident's first name.

He worked hard to prove this true. He operated under the assumption that it is hard to vote against someone who calls you by your first name. Considering the consistency with which he was re-elected, over the span of nearly 30 years, his assumption is hard to argue against.

Watching him work the town on a lazy afternoon was either impressive or sickening, depending on one's perspective.

On this particular afternoon Murphy spotted Papy two blocks from Duval Street, treating locals as if they were his own family.

"Paulie, Marina," he said, touching a gentle hand to each of their backs as they walked around a corner.

Paulie carried a bag of groceries. Marina carried a small child, as a second child, no older than three, hopped playfully in front of them.

"Hello Bernie," Paulie said.

"So good to see you. Little Ricky is growing."

"He's sure becoming a handful," said Paulie.

"Are you doing well?" Papy asked.

"Well, it's always a struggle, isn't it," said Paulie.

Papy moved his arm up around Paulie's shoulder. "It is," he said. "It's always a struggle, isn't it. You come find me, if there's anything you need."

"Oh, no, we're okay."

"Come see me. I want the best for you."

Murphy felt a twisting disgust in his stomach as he watched the scene from down the street. Papy was buying their votes with kindness. Murphy also knew, though, that if the kindness didn't work, more persuasive measures were used.

Murphy turned the corner and walked away before Papy had a chance to notice him.

7

EVA

"I swear to god, no more sailors, not for me."

Rachel was pretty, looked about 20 years old, with a figure that would stop most men's hearts if she looked at you in a certain way.

Today her looks were tarnished, though. Over her left eye was a cut. Blood dripped down around the eye socket, and the skin around the eye was a deep shade of purple.

Eva dipped a towel in a bowl of water and gently touched the wet towel to the cut.

Rachel jerked away.

"Easy," Eva said.

"Be careful."

"That's a hell of a cut, Rachel. Did he hit you with his wedding ring finger, or something?"

"Hell, I don't even know," Rachel said. "I wasn't looking at what finger smacked me the hardest."

"Well, don't worry, honey. I won't let him back in here. His days as a customer here are over."

"That goddamn bastard! No more sailors."

"He wasn't a sailor, Rachel. He was an admiral."

"Ain't that the same thing?"

No," Eva said. "If a sailor hits you, I can go complain to the admiral, and maybe the sailor gets talked to. If an admiral hits you, you can't go complain to the admiral, 'cause he's the admiral, and he's also the one who hit you."

"What the hell are you talking about?" Rachel asked.

"Never mind," Eva said.

A knock tapped rapidly at the door.

"It's open," Eva yelled.

The knob turned, and Cranston and Walter entered the room.

"Look, Rachel," Eva said, her voice thick with sarcasm, "the cavalry is here. We're saved."

"What happened to her?" Cranston asked, looking toward Rachel.

"Well," Eva began, "after paying for her services, an admiral who shall remain nameless, of our fine navy, decided he didn't respect Rachel much. Decided he had to let her know who's the boss."

"Bastard!" Rachel muttered angrily.

"What'd you do?" Cranston asked.

"What-yu mean what'd I do? I did whatever the hell he asked me to do. Every perverted, twisted thing. And for that I got smacked."

"Well," Cranston said, "we got some important things to discuss with Eva, here, so whyn't you ske-daddle."

Rachel looked at Cranston with contempt. Eva saw it and decided to ease Rachel off.

"Careful, Rach-," Eva said. "He ain't the one who smacked you."

"Is it all men?" Rachel asked.

"I don't think so," said Eva, "but the jury's still out."

Cranston cleared his throat impatiently. Walter, who had been taking in the scene in his usual quiet manner, made a point of pulling the door further open, and looking at Rachel.

"So," Cranston said. "About that ske-daddlin'…"

"You keep this bandage on for tonight," Eva said. "Come see me first thing."

Rachel stood silently, staring Cranston down. "Alright," she said finally. She walked past Cranston, eyeing him threateningly. Finally she was out the door, and Walter closed it quickly behind her.

Eva stood and tied a sash around her robe.

"Drink?" she offered.

"Wouldn't mind," said Cranston.

"Walter?"

"Whiskey."

Eva poured the drinks.

She set Walter's drink next to him on a side table. As she turned to Cranston, she gave him a look he could not quite handle, a flirtatious look. Cranston coughed and tried awkwardly to act comfortable.

"Thanks," he said, taking the drink from Eva.

"What can I do for you two fine gentlemen?" she asked.

"Well," Cranston stammered. "Eva, we have, uh, we have a few questions for you."

"Fire away," she said, lounging back into her easy chair and showing Cranston a small flash of naked thigh.

Walter noticed what Eva was up to and waved Cranston off. "When do you expect to see Trumbull?" he asked coldly.

"I don't," Eva said.

"When did you last talk to him?"

"I don't know when it was. The last time he was here. He drove off. I haven't talked to him since."

"On the telephone?" Walter asked.

"Nope. Nothing."

Walter eyed Eva suspiciously. Cranston decided it was finally his turn to talk.

"How about Diego Rodriguez?"

"Who the hell is Diego Rodriguez?"

"Now come on," Cranston said. "I know you know who Diego Rodriguez is. You get The Miami Herald here. You saw Trumbull's column. Don't play dumb with me."

Eva laughed. "Is that the poor joker he took out on the boat? He deserves anything he's got coming, especially from Trumbull. What, you think I'm gonna protect that sorry son-of-a-bitch? Find him. Do what you want with him. What the hell do I care?"

Walter was not impressed with Eva's sarcasm. He looked intently at her from under the brim of his hat. "We think you know a lot more than you're letting on."

Eva smiled cynically at the two men and shook her head slowly. "Search the place," she said.

Walter did not move. He stood looking at Eva.

"If Trumbull turns up," he said, taking an overly dramatic pause, "give him a message."

"Look, I don't expect to see him, okay. If he does turn up, I'll be too busy telling him what a bastard he is to give him any message from you. You can figure out how to give Trumbull your own message."

Eva, Walter, and Cranston stood silently, looking at each other.

Finally Walter turned toward the door and opened it. He was gone without saying anything.

Cranston tipped his hat awkwardly and said, "Eva." He turned to leave.

Eva smiled, whacked him on the butt and said, "Looking good, Cranston."

Cranston was out the door quickly. Eva laughed to herself quietly as she closed the door.

8
The Burning Man

Murphy typed with a halting rhythm, stopping periodically to stare at nothing, then turning back to the typewriter to tap out another sentence.

Carina stood to the side of her desk arranging knick knacks around her 'inbox' and 'outbox.'

Murphy and Carina were feeling more comfortable together.

Murphy stopped typing. He looked at the paper in the machine and thought for a moment. He sighed. He rested his chin in his hands and thought.

Then the door opened and Trumbull entered.

"Can I help you?" Carina blurted anxiously.

Trumbull looked from Carina to Murphy and laughed.

"Murphy, you sly dog. What kind of hanky panky are you puling here?"

"Hills hired her," Murphy said defensively.

"I'm Trumbull," he said, extending his hand to Carina.

"Oh, yes, Mr. Trumbull, of course."

"Not bad," Trumbull said, looking around the room. "Small."

"What do you need…to work?" Murphy asked. "We only have to the two desks."

"I'll work at the hotel," said Trumbull. "What's that you're working on?"

Murphy pulled the unfinished paper out of the typewriter and handed it to Trumbull. "There are some funny business deals going on," he said. "Somehow Papy bought several parcels of waterfront front property for one dollar."

"That's beautiful. One dollar," Trumbull said.

"No one's talking, of course. I'm having a hard time squaring the details. Did the county own the land? Did the state? It's a jigsaw puzzle."

Something lit up the room from outside, and Murphy, Trumbull and Carina turned at the same moment.

Flames danced outside, several yards in front of the building. Shock landed on all three, as they gazed through the window.

Outside, stuck deep in the grass, was a pole. The pole was bent at a ninety degree angle at the top, projecting a horizontal portion sideways. Hanging from the horizontal portion was a short human-shaped dummy. The dummy was made of straw and wrapped in newspaper.

The dummy was burning quickly, pages of the newspaper disappearing in heat and ash.

In less than a minute the effigy had burned out and nothing remained but the bent pole, and a blackened section of hanging rope.

Carina was frozen. Murphy was slack-jawed. Trumbull turned calmly away from the window and thought for a moment.

"Carina," Trumbull said, "Why did you want this job? Did you think it was going to be all high-minded reporting and heroics?"

Carina turned slowly away from the window, and away from Trumbull. "No," she said. "I wanted the job, because I wanted to be one of the boys."

Trumbull looked sideways at her. He turned to Murphy and whispered, "Not a bad answer."

Murphy was still looking out the window. "Someone called here the first day," he said. "Asked if I was the reporter they're going to hang."

"What did you say?"

"I said if they're going to hang a reporter it would probably be me."

"Good answer," said Trumbull. He turned back to the window. "Well, congratulations. They've noticed we're here."

9
Wisteria

Papy opened the door to his hotel suite, still wearing his pajamas, bathrobe and slippers.

"Come in, Frank," he said.

Frank Lester entered and shook hands with Papy. Papy put his arm around Frank Lester's shoulder and patted him on the back.

"How have you been?"

"Wonderful, wonderful," Lester said, in that business-speak that hides the truth as deeply as possible.

"So good to see you again."

"When you called I was delighted to hear from you."

"How are the wife and kids?"

"Wonderful. Couldn't be happier."

"Great. That's great. Oh, forgive my appearance," Papy said." Not exactly business attire."

"No, no," Lester said, sinking into a plush sofa. "It's your castle, Papy. When in Rome, and all that."

Papy set two glasses on the small table between them, and poured bourbon into each glass. He offered Lester the bourbon and said, "Thanks for coming."

"Not at all, not at all. The pleasure's mine."

"Well," Papy said, sinking into an arm chair opposite Lester. "Let's get down to business, shall we."

"Let's," said Lester. "What's cooking?"

"Wisteria," Papy said.

Frank Lester looked at him questioningly.

Wisteria Island sits across from Key West, a small island, reachable only by a short boat ride.

"Doesn't the navy own Wisteria?" Lester asked. "Don't they dump their garbage on it?"

Papy smiled. "I'll take care of the property deed. The navy doesn't necessarily own it."

"How are you going to pull this off, Papy?"

"Don't worry about that," Papy said confidently. "Let's skip ahead to your part of this."

"What's my part?" Lester was beginning to feel a bit concerned.

"The part where you make money hand over fist," Papy said.

"What do you have up your sleeve?" asked Lester.

"I'm already having Davis draw up the papers. By a few weeks from now, I'll own Wisteria Island. Just trust me on this. Then we clean up the navy's garbage, and begin building a top class resort."

Lester thought for a moment. "I do like the idea," he said. "I suppose my only concern is – "

"Let me handle the details," Papy interrupted. "If you like the idea of building the best damn resort, on a beautiful little island a five minute boat ride from Key West, running the whole operation in-house, making all that money without breaking a sweat, if that sounds good to you, then let's just agree in principle and sign the papers in a few weeks."

"You're a hard man to resist, Papy."

"Then don't resist." Papy smiled broadly.

Frank Lester smiled back. There was a note of uncertainty in his smile. He raised his glass toward Papy.

"To cooking the books!" Papy said.

"To cooking the books," Lester echoed.

10
The Offer

The knock sounded tentative. Judge McCarthur looked toward the door but did not say anything. He cocked his ear, listening.

The knock repeated, louder this time.

"Yes," McCarthur said.

The door opened and Gordon Davis entered the judge's private chambers.

"I appreciate your knocking," McCarthur said.

Davis stood just inside the door. "Is this a good time? You have a minute?"

"You're already in!" the judge blurted. "Close the damn door before someone sees you."

Davis closed the door and walked to the large chair facing McCarthur's desk. He sat on the chair. "The trial's just a month away, now," Davis said.

"It is that," said the judge.

Davis reached inside his coat and pulled a piece of paper out of his pocket.

He took a moment to straighten the piece of paper, making it look as neat as possible. Then he stood, side-stepped the table, and set the piece of paper in front of the judge.

McCarthur looked down at the paper, adjusting his reading glasses.

He peered out toward Davis. He did not say anything at first.

"It's a good offer," Davis said. "It's fair. Let us win the case."

McCarthur enjoyed making Davis – and by extension, Papy – squirm.

"I'll take it into consideration," McCarthur said.

"It's a good offer," Davis repeated.

McCarthur looked out over his reading glasses at Davis. "I said I'll take it into consideration."

78

Davis stood awkwardly in front of McCarthur.

"Is there a problem?" Davis asked.

"Mr. Davis," McCarthur said, "when I say I am taking something into consideration, I mean exactly that. I need some time to look at this issue."

Davis realized he was being toyed with. "Good day, your Honor," he said.

"Yes," McCarthur said, "It is a good day."

Davis retreated to the door, opened it, and left.

11
I want to hate you

Eva opened the door and looked out at Trumbull in the hallway. She didn't say anything, didn't give him any facial expression. Trumbull looked back at her the same way. No expression. No emotion.

It was a game of emotional chicken, and she didn't want to be the first one to crack.

She dropped her head and closed the door on him.

She returned to her chair and sat, putting her hand to her forehead.

He did not knock again, but he was still there. She could tell.

She breathed a heavy sigh and turned her head toward the door. The suspense was killing her. She cracked.

She stood and walked back to the door. She opened it. He was still standing exactly where he had been. She didn't want to look at him. She left the door open and turned back to the room. As she walked away from him, Trumbull entered and closed the door.

They didn't say anything to each other. Trumbull let her twist in the wind. He poured himself a drink and stood silently, looking in her direction.

In a sudden burst she grabbed a pillow and threw it violently at him. He ducked, holding the drink carefully. A tear ran down her cheek, but she wiped it away and collected herself.

"God damn you, Trumbull!"

Trumbull took a drink and looked at her. "Just like old times," he said.

Eva looked away from him and stared at the floor. "I want to hate you."

"It's not hard. A lot of people do."

"Why are you here? To see me, or to ask questions about Papy?"

"Can't I do both?"

"No." She looked back up at him. "You have to choose, me or your job."

Trumbull set his glass down on a bureau and walked toward her. He sat in the chair opposite her and waited a moment.

"How's Diego Rodriguez doing?" he asked.

Eva decided she could play the game along with him, and said, "He's doing great. Any day now he's gonna run for mayor."

Trumbull allowed himself a slight smile and eyed her appreciatively.

"What are you doing tonight?" he asked.

"Why?"

"Let's get together, talk, try a fresh start."

"Where?"

"You name the place," he said.

"The Boat Bar."

"Like old times," said Trumbull.

He stood up and moved toward her. He placed his hand on her cheek and then walked away toward the door.

"You're beautiful, Eva," he said. He opened the door and left, leaving Eva to stare blankly at nothing, wondering why she couldn't just tell him to go hell, once and for all.

12
Boat Bar Redux

Teddy, the bartender, saw Trumbull come in the door, and had a scotch on the rocks ready before he reached the bar.

The Boat Bar was noisy, energetic, full of hope and high expectation. The poker table had five people around it. The roulette wheel spun freely, giving the players the illusion of promise.

Tables around the bar were full of life and laughter.

Trumbull sat on the bar stool and thanked Teddy. He took a sip and looked toward the poker table. Amateurs, he thought, scornfully.

When Eva opened the door and walked in, Trumbull set his glass down on the bar, and gave her a faint nod. She was a vision.

Trumbull's struggle regarding Eva was a simple one; he wanted to be done with women. He wanted the freedom and peace of mind that only comes with being single. He also wanted Eva.

She walked toward him through the noise and clatter of the Boat Bar, and for just a split second he was taken back to the first time they met. She had impressed him from the start. A strong woman who still likes strong men. He appreciated her sarcasm and independence.

She sat on the bar stool next to him and asked Teddy for a whiskey.

As Teddy placed the drink in front of her, she took it, shifted toward Trumbull on the stool, and said, "I'm breaking up with you, Trumbull."

He froze for a moment. "I didn't know we were hitched," he said.

"There's a lot you didn't know," she said. "That's the problem."

"How can you break up with me, if we're not together?"

"Because I have to have some control over my own emotions."

"Come on, Eva," he said. "This doesn't suit you. You run a whorehouse. You're supposed to hate men. You're supposed to roll your eyes and shake your head. You don't care about all this silliness. That's for regular folks."

"You're right," she said. "I'm never surprised by anything men do, even you. Nothing surprises me. So I don't know why it bothers me so much when you act sweet on me, and then you drive away, and god knows how long until I'm going to hear from you again. You're different from the clowns my girls do business with. I guess, after all is said and done, I'm just another lonely girl."

Trumbull stared at the floor silently. Then he looked up at her. "You know we just opened a bureau here. I'll be around a little more."

"Yeah, that's great," Eva said. "Except there's one problem. I just broke up with you."

Trumbull smiled into his drink. "Okay," he said. "I guess it'll be okay if I'm just a reporter now."

"Fine," said Eva. "I have work to do." She stood and walked away from him.

Trumbull watched her swing her hips, sashaying into a crowd of sailors from Boca Chica who had just washed in the door.

First of the month, Trumbull realized.

He turned back to Teddy and asked for another scotch.

Then Trumbull recognized Walter making his way through the kitchen out to the front of the bar.

Trumbull watched as Walter made the rounds around the tables. He walked calmly, slowly, taking in everything, every amateur gambler, their habits, their intelligence, their tolerance for alcohol.

Finally Walter stopped at the poker table, his back to Trumbull. He watched the game for a minute, and then turned around. He had known Trumbull was there the whole time, but had not looked directly at him.

Trumbull raised his glass in a subtle 'hello.' Walter did not acknowledge the gesture. He walked to the darkened corner of the room where he always oversaw the proceedings and sat down.

"Whad'yu think, Teddy?" Trumbull asked the bartender. "Should I go say hi to Walter?"

"Hell no," Teddy said. "And now is when I stop talking to you, myself."

Teddy wiped the bar down in a show of busy-work, and then buried himself in the menial task of arranging glasses on a shelf.

Trumbull looked into the darkness of Walter's corner.

There was someone new there, a figure he did not recognize, large, a new enforcer, perhaps?

Trumbull set his glass on the counter and stood up from the bar stool. He walked toward Walter's corner. Along the way, over-eager sailors jostled him. He stayed focused on his target. Finally he was past the crowd.

Walter looked at him dispassionately. The large gentleman stood next to Walter eyeing Trumbull.

"How's things, Walter?" Trumbull asked. "Wanna introduce me to your new buddy?"

The large man seemed to grow an inch taller, and his more than ample muscles flexed.

Walter looked directly at Trumbull, and said, "You have a hell of a nerve, Trumbull."

"Yes, I suppose I do," Trumbull said. "It shouldn't be that strange. People shouldn't be so scared of everything."

"Be careful," Walter said. "I'm not throwing you out right now, but that doesn't mean it won't happen."

"Do it," Trumbull said. "Give me something juicy to write about. You been reading my column?"

Walter didn't answer.

"Who's the tree trunk?" Trumbull asked.

The large man tried to look as threatening as he could and said, "Name's O'Doole. Don't make me lose my temper."

"You're just the replacement, O'Doole. I'm not scared of you. I've dealt with the guys who came before you."

O'Doole clenched his fist and moved toward Trumbull. Walter waved him off.

"O'Doole!" Walter's voice echoed with command.

O'Doole eased off. Walter turned back to the room and eyed a sailor at the roulette wheel.

Trumbull touched his hand to his hat and said, "Good to meet you, O'Doole. We'll have to do this again. Your boss seems to have learned a small lesson. There's nothing you can do to me that won't come back and bite you in the ass. Just ask him about a guy named Diego Rodriguez."

Trumbull nodded one more time and turned away.

He was swallowed up by the crowd of gamblers and sailors, squeezing his way through the crowd toward the door. As he passed the roulette wheel, he suddenly found himself pinned against Eva, as she danced with a half-drunk sailor.

She noticed him and kept dancing.

"Trumbull," she said, dancing as she spoke. "This is Ensign Parkinson."

"Pleasure ," Trumbull said dryly.

"Ensign Parkinson is from Idaho."

"Long way from home," Trumbull said.

Ensign Parkinson was not sure what to make of Trumbull's sudden presence, so he decided to keep his mouth shut, keep dancing, and stay as close to Eva as he could.

"Come by the hotel later," Eva said. "Check out the girls. Maybe you'll find someone you like."

Trumbull looked at her. "No thanks," he said. "Try some other poor sucker. There's plenty to choose from."

Then he turned and walked out.

13
Diego is alive and well

Dear Cuz;

It's a reunion. I'm out on Old Jonah's boat again. Me, Jonah, and Diego Rodriguez.

Yes, he's alive and well. That is to say, he's alive. He isn't feeling well today. It seems he's been over indulging in a particular medicinal beverage that can bite as much as it can cure.

Diego is alive, anyway, which warms me inside. And you know what a sentimental fool I can be about old friends.

You may remember our last trip, the one where Diego Rodriguez insisted on showing Old Jonah and myself the secret resting places of former Key West Police Chief Darrel Martins, as well as his old partner in crime, Raul.

Today, though, we're just fishing.

The fishing's good. Jonah hauled in a marlin. Good size, not too big. Diego can handle a rod and reel himself.

Diego says he's scared to get off the boat when it docks. Says there's a few people looking for him who want to rough him up a little. But, just like last time, I've assured him that he has nothing to worry about. Papy and Walter and the rest of the gang have bigger problems.

Papy's going to be on trial in a month. It seems that pesky little matter of buying votes in the state assembly just won't go away. He bought off his colleagues and beat the censure vote, but I doubt he has the guts – or the wherewithal – to try something that transparent in court.

Then there's this troubling matter that my colleague Murphy has been digging up.

Papy has been buying up public land.

He's been rigging property deeds so he can take over prime real estate on the cheap. Some of it he's been buying from Monroe County, which doesn't even seem to own the land.

There you go. Papy's latest pick-pocket maneuver for all to see.

So I'm telling Diego to make a few public appearances. Walk around a little. Have dinner in a restaurant.

Papy can't touch him.

Papy has me to worry about.

-Trumbull

14
Chess Match

"This has to stop!"

Papy threw the newspaper at Davis and stormed around the hotel room, directionless.

"I agree, Pap," Davis said, conjuring up that calm tone of voice he used only when Papy was about to burst an artery.

"I mean, what do I have to do? Why are they persecuting me?"

"Pap," Davis said, "there's a right way and a wrong way to handle this."

"Right, we pull out all the stops. We go after Trumbull. Trumbull disappears."

"No, Pap, come on, think about this."

"We burn their new 'Miami Herald Key West Bureau' to the ground. We string up this – this – what's his name, Murphy? We string him up by his gonads until he sings soprano –"

"Pap!" shouted Davis.

Davis was perhaps the only person in the world who could raise his voice at Papy. He had done it only three times previously in the entire time they had known each other. On those rare occasions when he did raise his voice, Papy listened.

"Pap," Davis said, more calmly, "This is a chess match. We have to be at our most creative and clinical."

"What the hell do you mean?" Papy asked.

"Trumbull is a smart guy. He's playing a game with us. But to beat him - and we're going to beat him – we have to be smarter than him."

Papy was pacing around the hotel room anxiously. "I don't know, Davis. I don't want to appear weak."

"It's not weakness, Pap. It's winning. We have to beat Trumbull at his own game. Look, this is America, we can't just go burning down newspaper buildings. Maybe we should be able to do that, Pap, but we can't."

"They've been on this witch hunt for too long now. What did I do? Hm? Answer me that, Davis. What did I do to put these damn journalists against me? Did I miss the school play? Did I forget to tithe at Sunday school? What? What the hell did I do?"

"Pap, sit down. Let's think this through. We have angles we can play here."

Papy continued standing across the room from Davis.

"Have a seat," Davis said.

Slowly, Papy moved to the chair and sat. Davis sat facing him.

"So," Davis began, "first we think from their perspective. What do they get out of writing about you?"

"Readers!" Papy barked scornfully.

"Readers," Davis repeated. "Exactly, they get readers. So, what's the best way to get the readers on your side?"

Papy sunk his head into his chest, thinking. "We get them to write nice things about me."

"Jackpot," said Davis.

"How? How do I get these jackasses to write anything nice about me?"

"That," said Davis, "is the million dollar question. If we can answer that, if we can find a way to get them to WANT to write nice things about you, we win."

The Great Benefactor

Three sheets of news copy were stacked loosely on Murphy's desk. A half-written sheet sat idly in the typewriter. Murphy stared at the half-written sheet blankly. Next to him, twisted sideways in a chair, Trumbull absently tossed a baseball in the air and caught it. He tossed it again, this time freezing his movements as it returned to his hand.

"What plans does the navy have for Wisteria?" Trumbull asked

"The statement they gave me was a fuel depot," said Murphy.

"A fuel depot." Trumbull twisted his face and rotated the baseball absently in his hand.

"According to official navy records, President Coolidge, way back in the 20's, designated Wisteria for the navy. They just haven't done much of anything with it yet."

"So how does Papy get away with saying the county owns it? That's an even bigger stretch than taking this beach front property away from the state."

"Well," Murphy leaned back and spoke while looking up at the ceiling. "Maybe President Coolidge designated the island for the navy, but the county already had a claim on it."

"There would have to be some sort of deed dated from the twenties," Trumbull said.

Murphy laughed. "You think they'll provide one? A deed dated 1925 but on crisp new paper?"

"Wouldn't put it past them."

A few feet away the phone on Carina's desk rang.

"Miami Herald Key West Bureau." Carina had almost turned the greeting into a song. "MmHm, yes, would you like to speak to him?...Okay, one moment."

Carina put her hand over the telephone receiver and turned to Murphy. "Someone from Key West City Hall, wants to speak with the local editor."

"Is that what you are?" Trumbull snorted. "The editor?"

"Thanks, Carina." Murphy ignored Trumbull's sarcasm and rose to take the phone from Carina.

"Murphy here," he said. "Mmhm…okay…what time?...yeah, thanks."

Murphy hung up the phone and looked at the wall clock across the room. "You want to attend a 'major announcement by Bernie Papy' at City Hall?"

Trumbull sat up sharply. "Do I?" he snorted.

Trumbull and Murphy grabbed their hats and looked at each other.

"They invited us," Murphy said.

"They did that," said Trumbull. "They took the time to call. Something's fishy."

"Well," shrugged Murphy, "I'd rather go down working, than any other way."

Carina looked up from her desk with a note of worry.

"Don't worry, Carina," Trumbull said. "It's me they're after more than Murphy here."

Carina put her hand to her mouth. Murphy looked at Trumbull, amused and annoyed at the same time.

"Nothing's going to happen," Murphy assured her. "Not at City Hall.'

And the two reporters were out the door.

Fifteen minutes later they were blending into the back of a crowd of 40 people in a large atrium inside the Key West City Hall building. There was a buzz to the crowd. People were chatting in excited tones. Murphy and Trumbull stood at the back of the room taking it in, wondering what the quickly planned occasion had in store.

Then, through a door on the left side of the large room, Papy appeared and began shaking hands and patting people on the back. Hands went to shoulders. Papy worked the room as only Papy could.

Another ten minutes passed before Papy reached the front of the room. It was almost too much for Trumbull to take.

Finally, Papy stood behind a microphone and said, "Hello, fellow Conchs."

A round of applause rang through the room at the mention of the locals' pet nickname for themselves.

"I want to thank you all for coming. I have an announcement that I'm sure all of you will find as exciting as I do. As many of you know, I have been blessed with the acquisition of several wonderful pieces of local property, reasonably priced, beautiful parcels of God's most beautiful land. I am not exaggerating when I say that it humbles me to be the caretaker of these delicate plots of nature."

Trumbull looked at Murphy and mimed the motion of throwing up.

Papy continued. "So it gives me the utmost pleasure to announce today that I will be donating certain select parcels of this land to a variety of our most valuable and important charities."

Approving cheers rose from the crowd.

Murphy's eyes widened in understanding, as he saw what Papy was doing.

"Please, please," Papy calmed the crowd. "Thank you, but honestly, I am not doing this for any sort of public recognition. I am doing it for one reason and one reason only, because it is the right thing to do. So, I am announcing here today that I will be donating the plot at 431 Mahogany Avenue to the Catholic parish with the sole intention of using it for an orphanage to care for and minister to the most unfortunate among us."

Cheers, this time, were mixed with approving gasps of appreciation.

"I am also announcing that I will donate five acres of our most delicate wilderness land to the local Keys Nature Society, to protect the land, to research it, to provide a safe haven for our local wild life, and to create a haven for untamed nature in its most natural habitat. We must take care to coexist with nature, to embrace its wildness, and to treat nature with the respect it deserves."

Another ten minutes later Trumbull and Murphy were back outside, and Trumbull felt that he might throw up for real.

"Does he really expect us to run that as is?" Trumbull asked.

"Let's head back to the office," Murphy said. "I'll do the write up."

Within minutes they were in the same chairs they had been in before. Murphy tapped away with purpose. Trumbull unscrewed the top of his flask and tipped it back.

"Okay," said Murphy, "here's the opening; Monroe County State Representative Bernie Papy announced this evening that he will donate certain parcels of land –"

"–Fraudulently acquired land," Trumbull interrupted.

Murphy looked up. "Do we have proof it's fraud?"

"Suspiciously acquired land," Trumbull said.

"Suspicious," Murphy stopped and ruminated. "Land that he acquired under suspicious circumstances."

"Careful," Trumbull said, "you're going to lose the reader."

Murphy clicked his red pen and wrote a note on the page. "Let me try it, anyway," he said. "Monroe County Representative Bernie Papy announced tonight that he will donate certain parcels of land, which he acquired under suspicious circumstances, to the local Catholic Parish, to be used as an orphanage –"

"You're gonna set the record for run-on sentences," Trumbull muttered.

"Right," said Murphy. "Okay – he will donate a parcel of land – which he acquired under suspicious circumstances – to the local Catholic Parish, to be use as an orphanage. He will also donate a second parcel of land to the local - what's it called, the Keys Nature Society?"

"Something like that," barked Trumbull. "Okay, good. Now, we're not going to comment on it. Just say it like that. Then we spell out that Papy's also making an offer to buy Wisteria Island from Monroe County, even though according to all public records available to these reporters, Monroe County does not own Wisteria Island. The United States Navy does."

Murphy replaced the paper in the typewriter and leaned forward. "We're going to have another burning reporter dummy out our front window tomorrow."

"Hey," Trumbull said, "how come we aren't mentioning that?"

Murphy looked at him and smiled. "You want me to? Tack it onto the end?"

"It happened. Why wouldn't we report it?"

The two men gave each other a purposeful look. Trumbull nodded at Murphy. Murphy turned back to the typewriter and began tapping.

Trumbull stood up. "Well," he said, "I think you have this, Murphy. I have other matters to tend to. I'll see you in the morning."

Murphy continued typing. He barely stopped long enough to look up as Trumbull was leaving. "Hm? Oh, alright, see you Trumbull."

Trumbull closed the door on him, and Murphy tapped away, a solitary figure at a desk, trying to do something he believed in, one word at a time.

16
Reconciliation

“I broke up with you,” Eva said, leaning against the half-open door.

“I’m not here to talk you out of it.”

Trumbull stood in the hallway, looking in at her.

She looked down, sighed, and pushed the door all the way open. “I would have preferred if you WERE here to talk me out of it.”

Trumbull brushed past her as he walked in through the doorway. “We need to talk about Papy’s trial.”

Eva closed the door and rolled her eyes. “Trumbull,” she said, “look at me. Here I am. I’m standing in front of you. I’m not some ‘source’ in a suit passing on information. I’m living breathing flesh.”

Trumbull’s glance hid a smile. He poured himself a drink. He looked at her. “I want to kiss you,” he said. “But we have to discuss Papy’s trial.”

With one hand on her hip, the other hand went to her head to deal with the on-coming headache. She dropped the hand from her head and walked across the room. She sat and said, “Okay, talk.”

Trumbull carried his drink to the chair and sat across from her. He set the glass on the small table. “Are you going to testify against Papy?”

“I don’t know,” she said. “I didn’t want to deal with that. I just wanted to enjoy having the business running.”

“I can understand that,” said Trumbull. “But the clock is ticking. The trial’s just a few weeks away now.”

“I still don’t know,” Eva said.

“You’re scared of being shut down again,” said Trumbull.

“And you? Don’t you ever worry about what Papy might do? Cut you in an alley again? Worse? Look what happened to Martins.”

95

"Yes," said Trumbull. "Something bad will happen to me again. I know that."

Eva looked at him. "You know that? How?"

"It's just something I know," he said. "It's a trade off. We're boxing Papy in. As his violence increases, so does his exposure. Eventually it won't matter whether I'm the one saying it. He'll go one step too far, and everyone will know."

"But will they care?" Eva asked.

Trumbull picked up his drink and took a sip. "That I'm a little less sure about."

"So…what, you're asking me to go down with you? Some grand sacrifice so maybe Papy bites it in the end?"

"Well," Trumbull shifted in his chair, "you are thinking about this in terms of the larger picture."

"The larger picture…" Eva trailed off.

"Eva, this requires bravery. This requires caring more about the truth than about your own little world."

"My what?"

"Sorry." Trumbull cleared his throat and tried again. "MY little world, anyone's little world. This is about doing something bigger than saving your skin. This is about doing something heroic."

"What is it with you guys who went through the damn war?" Eva asked. "You're spending the rest of your lives trying to equal some stupid battle, where you were lucky enough not to get blown to smithereens."

Trumbull turned away from her and took another drink. When he turned back to her, his expression was serious. "Good buddies of mine were not lucky enough," he said. "Brave men, blown to smithereens."

"Okay," Eva said. "How does this relate?"

"They are gone, but we still won the war."

"So you have to keep trying to win wars for the rest of your life?"

"Eva." Trumbull paused to collect his thoughts. "You have a very insightful mind. I'll grant you that. You understand things that maybe some of us don't quite understand. But you have to make a choice."

She exhaled heavily. She shook her head. "I get it," she said. "If I decide to testify against him, can it be secret? Can we keep it quiet until the day I'm on the witness stand?"

"It's not my trial," Trumbull said. "The FBI, the Justice Department is prosecuting him. You would have to talk to them about it."

"But the paper," Eva said. "Would you report it, that I'm testifying?"

Trumbull smiled appreciatively. "Good question," he said. "I could say you informed me of your decision on condition of anonymity."

"You know all the angles."

"It's an essential tool of my business."

Eva looked at the corner of the ceiling, contemplating her decision. She was quiet.

Trumbull took a drink and looked her.

A minute passed in silence.

Finally she dropped her head and breathed a heavy breath. "Of course I'll testify," she said. "How could I not? I wouldn't be able to live with myself."

Trumbull finished his drink and nodded. "I knew I could count on you."

She stood up and walked to him. "I'm going it regret it. At some point, that is. I know one day, in the middle of going through hell, I'm going to wish I didn't do it."

Trumbull stood to face her. "You're smart. You're as smart as I thought you were."

They were close to each other. Eva looked up at him. His gaze met hers and their eyes locked together.

"What was it you said before we started talking about that?" Eva asked.

"Hm? Oh, you mean that thing about wanting to kiss you?"

"Yes, that," she said.

"I thought you broke up with me."

"Don't be ridiculous," Eva said. "I would never do something that stupid."

Trumbull touched her cheek with his hand. "Then there's the problem I'm dealing with, that I am trying to swear off women."

"No," she said, chuckling quietly, "You wouldn't do something that stupid, either."

Then she grabbed his face delicately with both hands. She ran her fingers down his cheek and touched her palms to his chest. She moved toward him and gave him a slow, delicate kiss.

He grabbed her around the waist and kissed her more forcefully.

17
Fishing Accident

From down the block, where two drunken gentlemen stumbled, laughing into the night, you would not have seen Walter and O'Doole lurking in the shadows.

They were there, though, waiting for the drunken men to stumble past.

When the coast was clear, Walter and O'Doole walked down the block in the direction of the docks.

They were silent, two figures, shrouded in the dark of night, silhouettes against the occasional street light. They walked with purpose, but unhurried.

When they reached the docks, which were absent their usual daytime bustle and story-telling, they headed down past the first few wooden walk-ways, and turned onto a familiar one. There, five boats down, bobbing gently against the dock as the current lazily lapped against it, was Old Jonah's boat.

Walter and O'Doole stopped to look at the boat for a moment before Walter nodded, and O'Doole climbed aboard. Walter glanced left, then right, and quietly grabbed the rail of the boat, pulling himself over.

They looked toward the cabin. Walter walked past the wheel, touched the cabin door, and quietly pushed it open. It was pitch black inside. O'Doole removed a flashlight from his coat pocket and turned it on. The light from the flash shone blindingly into the cabin, catching sight of Diego Rodriguez's face.

Diego awoke instantly and covered his face against the blinding light. In another instant fear and panic took over. He pushed with his feet, forcing himself into a sitting position against the wooden wall of the boat cabin. He tried desperately to block the blinding light from his eyes. He gasped. His breath came in anxious fits.

After a few minutes he realized that he could go nowhere and that the blinding light was not going to leave his eyes. He tried to

99

see past the light, to the two silent figures standing, but all he could make out were shoulders and the faint silhouettes of hat brims.

He couldn't take the silence any longer. "Who are you?" he asked frantically.

O'Doole let the stream of light drop from Diego's eyes. Then he raised the flashlight to show Walter's face. Then he turned his hand to light his own face. Then he turned the light back on Diego.

Diego kicked awkwardly at the wall of the boat. Then he dropped his head and began a faint whimper.

"Shut up," Walter said.

Then no one said anything for a moment. Diego's breathing slowed. He relaxed, with that relaxation that comes only when you resign yourself to the horrible fate about to befall you.

"Fine," he said. "Just do it quickly."

"What we're about to do," Walter said coldly, "is not actually happening."

"What the hell are you saying?!" Diego wailed.

"You had a fishing accident," Walter said.

"What? What are you talking about?

"You had a fishing accident," Walter repeated. "You took the boat out alone. You hooked a big one. You fought with it. The line got tangled around your hand as the fish pulled the boat in circles. You did the best you could, but eventually the fish was stronger. He was pulling the boat. You couldn't get your finger out of the tangle of line. The pull was too much to take. In the end, the fishing line cut off your finger."

Diego stared past the flashlight, perplexed.

Then O'Doole reached into his coat and pulled out a hatchet, sharp, it's gleaming blade reflecting brightly as the flashlight caught it in its beam.

Diego's eyes opened wide and he pushed back harder against the wall of the boat.

"You're not going to make any noise," Walter said. "You had a fishing accident, and nothing else. Now shut up. Let's get this over with."

Walter removed a towel from his coat pocket and moved toward Diego.

Diego's resistance ebbed. He sat and let it happen.

Walter pushed him forward so he could tie the towel around his head, through his mouth. Diego gasped as the towel entered his mouth. Walter pulled it tight and tied it in back of Diego's head.

Then Walter pulled Diego's right arm out straight, uncurled his tense fingers and straightened his right index finger, pushing it down hard onto the flat edge of the nearby bench seat.

Walter positioned himself slightly to the left, continuing to hold Diego's arm down hard onto the bench.

O'Doole waited for Walter's signal.

Finally Walter nodded. O'Doole swung the hatchet hard, hitting its target cleanly. The finger fell lifeless to the floor, a small comical prop in a larger horror.

Diego breathed frantically. His eyes glazed. He bobbed back and forth silently. His eyes closed once, twice.

Walter smacked him on the side of the head. "Come on!" Walter barked. "Let's get you bandaged up.

18
Two For Two

The liquor bottles, the cigar smoke, and the same men sat around the large table where they had celebrated the dollar-deal.

This time they were joined by Frank Lester, who sat next to Davis, to Papy's right.

"Davis, you have the paperwork?" Papy asked.

Davis presented several papers, spreading them neatly on the table in front of him. "This one," he began, "spells out Monroe County's historical ownership of Wisteria Island. Important in case the navy files a claim. These are for you guys." He pushed a few papers across the table to Douglas and Henderson.

"This," he said, turning to Papy, "is for you to sign."

Papy took the sheet of paper from Davis and peered at it pleasantly.

"Good work as always, Davis," Papy said.

"Thank you, sir. And this," he continued, shifting sideways to Frank Lester, "is your part, giving you exclusive development rights, right to build, right to control transportation from Key West, blah blah blah. It's all in order."

"Excellent!" Lester shouted happily. "Papy, I don't know how you do it, but I sure enjoy doing business with you."

"And I with you," Papy said. "Let's all sign up here, and get this deal into the books."

Pens scraped across paper. Papers were shifted from one person to another. More scribbling of names and dates.

Then Papy lifted up the final, signed and dated contract, and proclaimed, "It's done! Gentlemen, I own Wisteria Island!"

"Cheers!" was the unison response from around the table. Glasses were raised and emptied. Backs were slapped, hands grasped, and smiles shared all around.

102

"Gentlemen," Papy said proudly, "we are two for two. Two excellent property deals planned, two excellent deals accomplished. Congratulations!"

19

That Would Be A First For A Man

"Why do we keep putting ourselves through this?" Eva asked, walking alongside Trumbull through his hotel lobby.

"I'll be back in two weeks this time," Trumbull said. "Wasn't that always the problem? You never knew when we'd see each other again?"

"I have this nagging feeling I shouldn't trust you," she said.

Trumbull turned toward her. "The Miami Herald Key West Bureau," he said. "Mean anything to you?"

"No. Nothing."

"Well it should."

"What?" Eva asked. "What should the Miami Herald Key West Bureau mean to me?"

"It should mean that I'll be working here. Not all the time, but soon, and often. I'll be back here maybe half the month. I'll be local, Eva. At least semi local"

She looked into his eyes and sighed heavily. She smiled. "Maybe there's a part of me that just can't believe something could go right."

They were outside on the sidewalk now. Trumbull's car pulled up and a valet jumped out. Trumbull cocked his head to the side and looked away. "I guess I'll just have to prove I ain't lying by coming back when I say I'll come back."

"That would help," Eva said.

"What? Doing what I say I'll do?"

"Yes," she said. "That would be a first for a man."

Trumbull tossed some odd luggage into the car and turned to her. "Don't be such a softy," he said. "Life's gonna get pretty damn tough for you in the next month or two."

She nodded. "Thanks for reminding me."

They stood close to each other silently for a moment. Then Trumbull muttered, "Ah, screw it. Eva, you're the best. You're one in a million." And he leaned in and gave her a kiss.

When they pulled out of the kiss Eva was smiling at him.

Trumbull bent down into the car and sat behind the wheel. They looked at each other again and he closed the car door. He started the engine and drove slowly away from the hotel.

Driving away, Trumbull took a swig from his flask and looked back at Eva's fading figure in his rear-view mirror.

He had work to do.

She had to understand that.

She would understand that.

20
Shot Across The Bow

D ear Cuz;

I have a message for Papy: Not so fast!

He might control just about everything about Monroe County; the real estate, the water rights, the gambling, the money, you name it, he runs it.

But there's something he can't control, and that is the United States Navy.

It warms me inside to learn that the navy has filed a complaint in federal court stopping him from developing Wisteria Island. He hoped no one would notice, that the navy would shut up and keep to themselves. It seems, though, that the United States Navy is serious about its ownership rights. It doesn't take kindly to someone coming along and declaring ownership of something they already own.

Good job, sailors! You make an ex G.I. proud.

Another thing that has not gone unnoticed is Diego Rodriguez' missing index finger.

He didn't want to talk about it, but it sure was missing.

We were out fishing, myself and my new favorite fishing buddies, Jonah and Diego. Diego didn't want to talk much that day. He was quiet. Just wanted to tend the lines. I could tell something was bothering him, though, something he didn't want to talk about.

When I asked him about the missing finger, he shrugged and said it was a fishing accident. I probed for more information. He said he took the boat out alone and his finger got caught in a line.

I don't buy it. Jonah laughed when he said he took the boat out alone. Jonah has a good laugh. It comes out whenever someone is telling a lie. Jonah said Diego never took the damn boat out alone, and he never lost his finger in any fishing accident.

Diego wouldn't talk about it anymore, though.

I don't know about you, but I believe Jonah on this one.

Diego never took the boat out alone. He lost his finger alright, but not in a fishing accident.

It's alright. I don't plan to press Diego on it much right now. I like Diego. I'll get him talking one of these days.
-Trumbull

Episode Three:
Papy On Trial

1
Doing the Smart Thing

Eva stood in front of the mirror over her bureau. The business card lay among other papers. She stood with her back to Walter and Cranston.
Eva looked down at the business card.
It said:

> Stephen J. Trumbull
> The Miami Herald

She picked up the card and looked at the back, where Trumbull had written his home phone number in Miami, as well as his address.

She turned slowly toward Walter and Cranston.

She held out the card and walked a few steps toward them.

"Smart move," Walter said, taking the card and putting it in his pocket.

"Now, about your testimony," Cranston said. "We'd like you to meet with the attorney who's gonna be defending Papy."

"When?" Eva asked.

"Tomorrow. He'll be wanting to organize and plan what you'll be saying up on the witness stand."

"What, he's going to write me a script? Plan a rehearsal and everything?"

"We just want, uh, our uh, our message," Cranston stammered, "to be, well, what's the word?"

"Crafted?" said Eva.

"Crafted, yes," Cranston agreed. "Everybody should be on the same page in Papy's defense."

Walter raised his head and leaned forward. "Eva," he said, "we know you were planning to testify against Papy. Don't bother asking. We just know." He paused and looked directly at her. "You're doing the smart thing."

Walter and Cranston stood and turned toward the door.

Cranston tipped his hat just slightly and said, "As always, Eva, it's, it's a, uh, a pleasure."

Eva smiled at him and said, "You sly dog, Cranston. No woman could ever resist you."

Walter opened the door, and Cranston nearly walked into it, side-stepped it, and left awkwardly.

Now alone in her room, Eva put her hand to her head and breathed a heavy sigh. She stood this way for some time, thinking. Then she turned, sat in a chair, lifted the phone from its receiver, and began to dial.

2
Your Move

Trumbull sat at the small table that served as a dining table in his under-used dining room. Light came down dimly from the weak overhead bulb. Newspapers were spread out in front of him.

He took a sip of his drink and turned the page of the newspaper.

Most of Miami was asleep.

Trumbull heard faint sounds outside his door.

He looked up at the door. He did not move.

His eyes closed as he listened quietly for the sounds to return.

The door knob began to rattle.

Trumbull reached up and pulled the string that turned off the overhead bulb.

The sound of hardware monkeying inside the lock prompted Trumbull to stand up and step quietly into the pantry.

Everything was pitch black.

Then the rattling of the door knob stopped and slowly, quietly, the door to Trumbull's apartment opened.

He was not sure how many there were. Three, maybe four people.

Then a flashlight erratically lit parts of the room, and Trumbull squeezed into the corner of the pantry where he could still see out but could not be seen himself.

The beam from the flashlight whisked around the room.

Then it stopped on the table.

Trumbull's glass still sat there, ice not melted, scotch still alive. He was given away.

Whoever they were, they knew he was close. He had the advantage of home-court, though. They did not know where he was, and they did not know the layout of the apartment.

The man holding the flashlight stood in the center of the living room. He dropped the beam to the floor and began whispering instructions to the others.

The hand holding the flashlight rose to scratch an itch, and for a brief instant O'Doole's face was partially illuminated.

Trumbull nodded knowingly in the dark. Then he began planning his strategy.

His options were not great. They had him. The trick was simply to stay alive.

Trumbull calculated that he would have to go along with whatever O'Doole had planned. That, or end this in an ill-conceived massacre, an end that would no doubt include himself.

This was the moment when he understood what Eva had done.

He hadn't liked what she told him when she made the call. But now he understood.

Smart woman.

He just had to hope the FBI tail was on the level, and not another stooge of Papy's.

Trumbull stayed silent in the pantry corner, waiting for the right moment. O'Doole had sent the others down the hallway toward the bedroom and bathroom. O'Doole was alone in the living room. He sauntered aimlessly toward the small table.

He shined the flashlight on the glass. The ice cubes had cracked in the whiskey. O'Doole touched the outside of the glass, where droplets of moisture beaded.

He picked up the glass and raised it to his nose, sniffing the fine scotch aroma.

He took a sip.

"Set it down slow," Trumbull said, jamming the barrel of his revolver into O'Doole's back.

O'Doole froze. He set the glass down slowly.

"Reach up," Trumbull said. "Turn on the light."

O'Doole reached into the darkness, found the hanging string and pulled it.

Once again the bulb weakly lit the room.

The others were returning from the hallway to the living room. They stayed out of the light. Trumbull still didn't know how many. He kept the gun in O'Doole's back.

"Now here's how this is going to play," Trumbull said.

A voice came from the darkness of the living room. It was weak and tinny-sounding. "We'll be the one's dictatin' the play here," it said.

Trumbull raised his revolver and pointed it under O'Doole's chin.

"Frankie!" O'Doole barked. "Do what he says."

There was an awkward silence.

"So, as I was saying," Trumbull began, "here's how this is going to play." Trumbull stopped and peered into the darkness of the living room.

"There's a wall switch," he said. "Turn on the damn light."

A fumbling sound came from the living room. Then the light came on to reveal two men, one short and plump, the other thin and lanky. The men stood awkwardly, facing Trumbull.

"I don't know what you fellas have planned for me," Trumbull said, "but I guess it's time to find out. The only thing that isn't gonna happen here tonight, is that no one's gonna get killed. Not me, not O'Doole, here, and if you fellas are smart, neither one of you."

"How do you know you're not gonna get killed?" O'Doole asked, mockingly.

"I know it, because we're all being watched, right now. From the street. I got a tail on me day and night. Anything happens to me, you boys are cooked."

"We ain't afraid of no tail," O'Doole said.

"No?" asked Trumbull. "Well, we're all about to find out, aren't we. Now, I'm going to toss my gun down. You boys have me, alright. No one's going to lose their head and do something stupid. No one's going to bite it, cuz if anyone does, then we all probably do. You got me? You understand?"

Surprisingly, the weak tinny voice came from the short plump man. "We got it," he said tentatively.

Trumbull, O'Doole, the short plump man and the thin lanky man all stood facing each other. A moment passed.

Finally Trumbull pulled his revolver away from O'Doole, pointed it straight up, uncocked it, held it out in front of him, and tossed it to the floor.

"Your move," Trumbull said.

3
One of The Boys

The Miami Herald Key West Bureau was temporarily closed. The only two full-time employees of the bureau, Pat Murphy and his secretary, Carina, were in Tallahassee. Murphy would be covering Papy's trial and Carina had become inseparable from Murphy.

They had arrived earlier in the day after the long drive from Key West, checked into their hotel, and ordered dinner.

The several weeks that Murphy and Carina had known each other had brought them closer, but there remained a touch of awkwardness. Murphy showed affection toward her at times, but often pulled back into a professional aloofness that Carina found frustrating.

For her part, Carina felt nothing but tenderness for Murphy. She knew she needed to find that balance between her feelings toward him and their professional relationship, but she told herself she couldn't help how she felt, and so she was going to feel how she felt, and that was that.

She wasn't going to tell Murphy how she felt, though, until he said something first. After all, she told herself, there did have to be some sense of chivalry left in this crazy world.

After settling into Tallahassee, Murphy took Carina to a bar called Dutch, where he had shared drinks with Trumbull on one of their previous visits to town. He ordered a scotch – he had learned from Trumbull – and asked Carina what she wanted to drink.

"Scotch," she echoed, loud enough for the bartender to hear over the clatter.

For the next few hours they drank and talked and told stories. Carina told Murphy of her childhood, of growing up the only sister with four brothers, and how that had made her always want to be 'one of the boys.'

Murphy told her about his winding road through college to the field of journalism. He tried to wow her with his tales of

114

Trumbull's daring exploits. He realized, in the middle of his third Trumbull story, that he had no stories of himself that matched the drama of his Trumbull stories.

And it was around this time, as he was deep into his third Trumbull story, that he realized to his horror, that he had become decidedly more drunk than Carina. He came to this realization as his head spun slightly, and his attempt to relate a small detail of the Trumbull anecdote came out of his mouth in a slur of nonsense.

Carina smiled politely at him as he looked at her. Then she motioned to the bartender that she would pay the tab, which she did with The Miami Herald Key West Bureau's petty cash – which she had full control of.

Then she politely helped the drunken Murphy to his feet, and, supporting his right arm around her shoulder, helped him shuffle in the direction of the door.

"Oh, god," Murphy slurred, once they were outside. "oowwhut haf I dunnn?"

"You're alright," Carina said, seeming bright and lucid. "Let's get you to the hotel and into bed."

"Oh, you – you," but Murphy trailed off.

She supported him as they stumbled awkwardly for three blocks to the hotel.

Inside, she fumbled in his pants pocket for his room key, found it and opened the door. She dropped him onto the bed, and began removing his shoes and socks.

Moments later, after she had undressed him, she slid him long ways onto the bed, and covered him with the blankets.

She stood and stared at him for a moment, smiling and shaking her head, before turning around, walking out the door, closing it behind her, and crossing the hallway to her own room.

4
Followed

O'Doole drove the car through the dark Florida night, hunched over the wheel as if he expected something to jump out in front of the car at any moment.

In the passenger seat next to him sat the thin lanky man. Behind him was the short plump man. Trumbull sat to the right side of the back seat.

Trumbull stared out the car window as the darkness passed by. They had been driving for a couple of hours, and Trumbull had come to recognize – even in the dark – the long road along the Keys to Key West.

The four of them rode in silence as the night passed by outside. Trumbull turned from the window and looked at O'Doole in the driver's seat.

"Hey O'Doole," he said.

"What is it?"

"You think I could have my flask? It isn't loaded or nothin."

O'Doole did not answer right away. He stayed hunched over the wheel peering out at the road.

After a minute he glanced back at Trumbull, then looked sideways at the thin lanky man, and snorted, "Alright, give him his flask."

The thin lanky man twisted his arm back toward Trumbull and Trumbull took the flask out of his hand. He took a good swig and relaxed comfortably into the car seat.

The short plump man next to Trumbull said, "How come the only guy in this car actin' relaxed is the guy who's about to kick the bucket?"

"Frankie!" O'Doole snapped.

Trumbull turned to the short plump man and said matter-of-factly, "Until it happens, you can't say for sure that it's gonna happen."

"What the hell you mean by that?" the short plump man asked.

Trumbull did not answer. He turned back to the window.

"What the hell's he mean by that?" the short plump man asked to whoever was listening.

"Frankie," O'Doole said nervously.

"What?"

"Keep your head down, but keep an eye out the back window. Trumbull maybe was right. I think that car's following us."

Frankie hunched down and twisted backwards. He peered out the back window at two headlights. They were the only other headlights on the road, and they hung back several car lengths, keeping a steady, uniform distance from O'Doole's car.

"How long they been there?" Franky asked.

"I think since Miami."

"Well, lose 'em," Frankie said.

"Frankie, we're on a bridge. What do you want me to do? Drive off into the water?"

"Damn it!" Frankie said.

O'Doole stayed hunched over the wheel, but nervously turned to the rear-view mirror at increasing intervals.

Trumbull calmly took another swig from his flask.

"Alright," O'Doole said. "We're coming up on Long Key. Gonna pull off behind a gas station and see what they do."

They drove for a few more minutes and then O'Doole pulled off the road into a gas station parking lot. He hit the lights, darkening the already black car, and rolled to the back of the station.

They sat quietly for a moment.

"Here they come," O'Doole said.

A black sedan drove slowly past the gas station. It kept going, crawling deliberately through the night.

"They didn't stop," said O'Doole.

"You sure?" asked Frankie.

"They kept driving!" O'Doole said, somewhat annoyed.

"As long as we're stopped," Trumbull said, "I could use a restroom."

The men looked at each other in the dark.

O'Doole looked at the thin lanky man, and said, "You go with him. Keep the gun in your coat pocket. Aim it at him the whole time. He tries anything funny, shoot him." Then O'Doole added, "Don't kill him. Just put him in the hospital."

5
Dog and Pony Show

Papy paced behind a couch, more agitated than nervous. He was alone in the room, a modest chamber adjacent to court room B4. This was the court room presided over by His Honor, Judge Ian McCarthur.

Papy came to life as the door opened and Davis entered. Davis was followed by Stan Belmont, of Briggs and Belmont – Attorneys at Law. Belmont had known – and defended - Papy for more years than either of them cared to count.

"'Bout time," Papy said. "What took you guys?"

"Long story," said Davis.

"What's the skinny? What's going on?"

Stan Belmont navigated the semi-circle of couch, chair and coffee table, and approached Papy confidently. "Bernie," Belmont began, placing a calming hand on Papy's shoulder, "we're going to be alright in the end. McCarthur is playing this the only way he can."

"What, by taking whatever I offer, and still making me twist?"

Belmont looked at Papy warmly and patted his shoulder, motioning to the chair.

Papy grudgingly sat. Belmont and Davis sat across from him.

"Listen to me," Belmont said. "This is just procedure."

"Procedure, my ass!" Papy barked.

"Look, we have to go in there right now and plead 'not guilty.' We have to do this thing. It's going to work out okay. Trust me on this."

Papy gave his head a half shake and looked sideways at the lawyer. He turned to Davis and said, "Davis, you agree?"

"I do," Davis said.

Papy dropped his head in exasperation. A pregnant moment passed.

"Alright," Papy said. "Let's go."

119

Moments later, Papy, Davis, and Belmont were adjusting their chairs at the defendant's table when the door from McCarthur's private chamber opened.

"All rise," the bailiff said mechanically. "The Honorable Ian McCarthur presiding."

"Fine, fine. Sit down, everyone. Jesus!" McCarthur plopped heavily into his own chair and looked out at the room. "Well Christ Almighty," he said casually. "The whole damn state of Florida here?"

A stony silence greeted McCarthur from the packed room.

McCarthur looked from one side of the room to the other. Every seat was filled. The small overhead balcony was also packed. Court Room B4 had seldom known so many people.

McCarthur looked at the prosecutor's table. Three men, impeccably dressed in expensive tweed suits, sat smugly, awaiting McCarthur's instructions.

McCarthur turned to his left, to the defendant's table, looked first at Belmont, then moved on to Davis. Finally McCarthur looked directly at Papy.

"Representative Papy," McCarthur said. "You're entertainment. We should move this trial to the Gator's football stadium and sell tickets."

Papy lifted his head as if to respond but McCarthur put a hand up.

"For Chris'sake don't talk now. It wouldn't be appropriate. Bailiff, let's get this dog and pony show under way."

The bailiff rose with a piece of paper in his hands. He mechanically read aloud the charges against Papy, detailing Papy's alleged attempts to buy votes in the state legislature.

Papy, sitting stiffly between Davis and Belmont, stared blankly at the floor in front of the defendant's table. His ears tuned out the bailiff. All Papy heard was the sound of dozens of pens scratching across notepad paper behind him.

This sound grew in his consciousness, every pen scraping across paper, noting these charges, to be printed in newspapers the following morning, scraping, scraping, louder and louder, until he turned around suddenly, and his eyes met those of Pat Murphy three rows back.

An elbow struck Papy in the ribs. Papy looked down with a start. Davis was whispering.

"Pap! Pap!"

"Hm?"

"How do you plead?"

"Oh, uh, why, not guilty!" Papy said loudly.

Davis was looking at him with a note of concern.

"Let the record show that the defendant pleads not guilty," McCarthur barked. "Thank God for that. Otherwise we wouldn't have any fun."

6
Two Stories

Murphy and Carina fought their way out of the crowded court room as soon as McCarthur gaveled the proceedings suspended for the lunch hour. It took several minutes, but eventually they squeezed their way out into the hallway just in time for Murphy to grab the last wall phone.

He dialed Hills' number in Miami and waited for it to ring.

"Hills." The editor had lost his polite niceties years ago.

"Murphy here. Papy pleaded not guilty. You want me to write it up, or put Carina on with someone? So far it's nothing unexpected."

"Fine," Hills said. "I'll have Carina read her notes to Daniels in a minute. First, I have something to tell you."

Murphy was surprised by Hills' tone of voice, and reluctantly said, "What is it?"

Hills paused a moment before answering. "Trumbull's been taken."

"Ta – taken! What do you mean 'taken'?"

"Papy's guys took him in a car last night. It was around one in the morning. There's an FBI tail."

"Wh – what are we going to do? Do we know if he's alright?"

"He's alright so far," Hills said. "As a paper we're not going to interfere. I mean, you know, the FBI is on it."

"Can we trust them?" Murphy asked, the news beginning to cause a twist deep in his stomach.

"We think so," Hills said.

"You THINK so." Murphy looked up at nothing high above him and then dropped his gaze erratically.

"Murphy," Hills said calmly, "We're going to write about this while its happening. We're not going to interfere with the FBI, but whatever news they give us, we're printing. So tomorrow's

122

paper runs two front page stories. First, Papy pleads not guilty. Second, Papy's men kidnap Trumbull."

"I don't like it," Murphy said.

"Well no one likes it," Hills said. "The point is we write up the story and run it."

Murphy was at a loss. He stood dumbly, phone receiver to his ear for half a minute. Finally Hills could take it no more.

"You want to put Carina on?" He asked. "I'll get Daniels. and they can put your court room notes together."

Carina took the receiver from Murphy's outstretched hand, gazing questioningly at him. She slowly put the receiver to her own ear and finally said, "This is Carina."

"Hold on a moment," Hills said. "I'll put Daniels on. Give him your court room notes."

7

The Mangrove Canopy

Trumbull awoke with a start. He was laying on the floor of a small rowboat, his head twisted sideways to the left of Frankie's feet.

He peered up. A canopy of tree branches and leaves obscured a partly cloudy sky. The boat he was in moved slowly, causing the canopy of branches to shift slightly, moving backwards above him. He blinked his eyes and raised his head. Sitting with his back to Trumbull at the front of the boat was O'Doole, steering the boat through a shallow channel by moving a long pole through the water. O'Doole was not so much rowing the boat as pushing it, stabbing the pole on the shallow bottom under the water, and slowly heaving the boat forward.

"Sleeping beauty is up," Frankie said.

O'Doole turned and looked down at Trumbull. Trumbull sat up on the floor of the boat and rubbed his eyes.

"What's going on?" he asked.

Then his memory began to clear. O'Doole and his two friends had been so spooked by the FBI tail that they were afraid to get back on the road. They had sat in the car, in the dark, arguing for two hours before O'Doole decided to hijack the small boat and disappear across Florida Bay in the night, into the wild Everglades.

"Where's whats-is-name?" Trumbull asked. "Stickman."

O'Doole and Frankie did not answer at first. Then O'Doole turned and said, "On his way to Key West to get Walter." Then he turned all the way around and looked directly at Trumbull. "You're precious cargo. We have plans for you."

"You had plans for me last night," Trumbull said, sitting upright and looking out at the passing mangrove forest. "Did they include being gator dinner?"

O'Doole and Frankie both stood up in a panic as they saw the 12-foot alligator Trumbull was referring to.

The gator peered up at the three of them from half-submerged eyes, bellowed a low belch, and swam away powerfully, disappearing into the thick vegetation.

"I don't like this," Frankie said.

"Don't act like a scared girl," O'Doole snapped. Gators don't attack unless they feel threatened."

"When did you become a park ranger?" Frankie asked.

"Hell, if you want I'll step into the damn water and pet the damn thing."

"Like hell you will."

Trumbull interjected with a calm, relaxed voice, "If you two are done wetting your pants, mind if I ask what you have planned for food?"

Frankie reached into a small bag next to him and pulled out a half sandwich wrapped in wax paper. "Ration it," Frankie said "It'll have to last you."

As Trumbull reached for the sandwich he suddenly became aware of the swarm of mosquitoes that seemed intent on devouring the three men. He waved his hand at the swarm, causing no particular damage to any of them.

At that moment the sound of an outboard motor cut harshly into the wild soundtrack, and O'Doole and Frankie instinctively ducked down into the hull of the boat.

Trumbull, however, stood up straight and, raising his hand to his forehead, peered through the dense growth trying to catch a glimpse of whatever vessel was passing by.

8
The Long and Short of It

"Representative Dubois," the lawyer said, almost in a sing-song voice. "You represent, correct me if I am wrong, the Twelfth District, in the Florida State Assembly?"

The man in the witness chair adjusted his round wire rim glasses, and said, "Yes."

"And how long have you represented the district?"

"I'm proud to say that the voters have been sending me back for twelve years now."

"And how would you characterize your voting record during those twelve years, as compared to, say, Representative Papy."

"Objection!" Belmont barked from the defendant's table. "Irrelevant."

"I intend to show," the lawyer began, turning to Judge McCarthur, "Patterns and tendencies that have led Mr. Papy to, uh, coerce his colleagues into voting certain ways."

McCarthur peered over his reading glasses at the lawyer. "Papy's not on trial for coercing votes, Mr. Landis. He's on trial for buying votes. Objection sustained." Then McCarthur turned to the defendant's table. "But don't get too cocky, Belmont," he said.

The lawyer exhaled deeply and turned back to Representative Dubois.

"Were there any occasions, Representative Dubois, when Mr. Papy offered you anything of substance, of value, in exchange for voting his way?"

"Absolutely."

"Would you care to describe these circumstances for the court?"

"Well." Dubois looked down, avoiding the intense gaze coming from Papy. "There was a bill Papy brought up, had something to do with water rights in the Keys. I didn't really have an opinion on it, one way or the other. I mean, my territory's up

126

here in northern Florida. What do I know about the Keys? So, this bill seemed to put Papy pretty much in charge of all the water rights down there. He wrote his self a bill putting his own companies in the driver's seat. The bill even spelled out men on the aqueduct board who were Papy's own men. Well, I thought it went too far. It was a blatant attempt to put his self on a throne, so to speak. So I came out against it."

A pause silenced the court room before Dubois continued.

"Later that night, as I'm leaving the building, walking down the hallway, Papy and some fella I didn't know come around the corner and stand in my way.

"At first I felt a little bit scared, naturally. If I didn't know better I'd have thought I was about to get mugged. Then they stops me and Papy says, 'Hello Dubois. How's the family?' I says, 'Doing good.'"

"Yes, yes, Mr. Dubois," the lawyer interrupted. "In what way did Mr. Papy attempt to, uh, procure your vote?"

"Well, first he tells me a bill of mine is dead. He just says it's dead, just like that. I had this bill, see, co-sponsored it, setting up oversight of corporate state taxes. Now maybe Papy didn't like my bill, but he just up and tells me it's dead. Then he changes his tone some and starts wheelin' and dealin' about how I could get a good committee appointment if I supported his damn water bill. Well I was kinda stunned. I didn't even give him an answer at first. Then he puts a cigar in my shirt pocket and tells me to go look at what's on my desk."

"Your desk," the lawyer echoed.

"Yeah, and I had just left my office. There couldn'ta been anything on my desk, s'far as I could figure."

"Did you go look?"

"I did."

"And what did you find there?"

"Two cases. A case of Cuban cigars, and a case of damn fine rum."

"So," said the lawyer, turning to project toward the court room. "Let me see if I understand. Mr. Papy promised you a committee appointment if you would vote for his water rights bill. Then he told you to go look on your desk, where you found a case of Cuban cigars, and a case of rum."

"That's about the long and short of it," Dubois said.

"And did you end up voting for Mr. Papy's water rights bill?"

Dubois squirmed in his seat. "I hate to admit that I did."

"And did you receive the committee appointment that Mr. Papy promised?"

"Yes, I did."

The lawyer turned to the defendant's table and said confidently, "Your witness."

Belmont stayed in his seat, smiling at Dubois on the witness stand. The court room was silent for a full minute. Finally, without standing, Belmont asked, "Did any money change hands between yourself and Representative Papy?"

"Money?" Dubois said.

"Yes, money." Belmont sat forward in his chair. "We are here to try my client for buying votes, as His Honor just stated. Did any money change hands in this exchange between yourself and my client?"

"Well, no, I can't say as any money changed hands, but he made it pretty darn clear – "

"Yes, yes, Mr. Dubois." Belmont was finally standing and approaching Dubois in the witness chair. "You have stated already that my client was, how did you put it, 'wheeling and dealing.' Mr. Dubois, how does a bill get written? How does a bill pass the Assembly? Is it all straight forward? It's either a good bill or a bad bill, and by gad, if it's a bad bill, why then I won't vote for it? Is it as simple as that Mr. Dubois? Or would you say 'wheeling and dealing' is in fact common practice in the day to day workings of any governmental body?"

"Well, now you're twisting my words."

"It's a simple question. Is wheeling and dealing part and parcel of the inner workings of government?"

"Well sure, but – "

"And you have said right here on the witness stand that no money changed hands between yourself and my client."

"Well, now – "

"Mr. Dubois." Belmont had found his groove. "We are here to discuss the issue of buying votes. You would sit in this witness chair and slander my client, Representative Papy, while at the same time, as a part of your own story, tell us that he inquired about the health of your own family, and presented the possibility of your own advancement up the rungs of government with a good committee appointment. Mr. Dubois, are those the words of someone who is trying to deceive you, or are those the words of a generous and kind man, intent on looking out for your own good?"

"Objection! Counsel is putting words into the witness's mouth." The lawyer looked at Judge McCarthur seriously.

McCarthur ruminated for a moment and said, "Sustained. Belmont, go easy on the flowery stuff. It doesn't become you."

"Your Honor," Belmont began, but McCarthur cut him off.

"Oh save it. You won this round. Hell, they made it easy for you. All due respect to you, Mr. Dubois, but you stunk this court room up just now. Dismissed."

9

Dumber'n a Bent Hubcap

"Paper! Paper! Papy pleads not guilty! Trumbull kidnapped! Paper!"

The boy stood on the corner across from Murphy's hotel in Tallahassee. He was doing brisk business. In a half hour he was sold out. Murphy turned from the window and sat at the room service cart, satisfied and purposeful.

Across Florida The Miami Herald disappeared from news stands in a hurry.

Judge McCarthur had bought one on his way to the courthouse, and was reading it at his desk, when the side door to his private chamber rattled with a nervous knock.

"Come in," he said tentatively.

The door opened and Davis entered, followed by Belmont. Belmont left the door open behind him as he entered.

"Close the damn – " McCarthur's voice halted in shock as Papy walked into the room and shut the door.

"Morning, McCarthur." Papy said.

"What in the name of good Christ are you doing in here?" McCarthur blurted.

"Your Honor," Papy began.

"Don't 'Your Honor' me. Holy mother of all things bent and narrow! Papy, I ain't supposed to speak with your council right now, but things being what they are I'll make an exception, but you, in case it happened to have slipped your goddamn mind, are the defendant in this here circus, and you being in here right now violates all things decent and just – if there are any of those things left in this world."

"Your Honor, drop this case. It's clear by now that there isn't any justification. You said so yourself yesterday. They made it easy."

130

"Of all the stupid-!" McCarthur began. "Papy, sometimes you're dumber'n a bent hubcap. If it weren't for Davis here I don't know how you survive."

"The case is without merit."

"What the hell difference does that make?" McCarthur yelled, instantly dropping his volume out of fear his voice would carry down the hall.

In Murphy's hotel room, the room service eggs were too salty and the coffee was not strong enough. Murphy's purposeful, satisfied demeanor had waned. He rose from his chair to answer the door, and found Carina outside.

"Morning, Carina. Come in."

"Hi." She pulled off her hat, and swished her hair in that way that made Murphy weak inside.

"Damn eggs are too salty," Murphy said. "You can have 'em if you want."

"No thanks. I ate," answered Carina. "I was down the street at the place we ate at yesterday."

"I might be headed there myself."

Carina casually twisted her head sideways and asked, "You have any idea why Papy would be at the courthouse this early?"

Murphy twisted his face and looked at his wrist watch. "You sure?" he asked.

"I was having my breakfast, sitting at the window, looking out at nothing, when his car pulling up caught my attention."

Murphy looked at Carina with surprise and admiration. "Carina, we're going to make a true journalist out of you yet. You're brilliant."

Murphy went to the desk and collected his wallet and a few odds and ends. He threw on a jacket and waved at Carina to follow him.

Three minutes later they were crossing the street in front of the courthouse, and walking quickly through the big glass double doors.

Murphy looked left then right, and saw what he was looking for; the floor plan of the building, with room numbers and judge's chambers marked.

He scanned the floor plan and the notations. He didn't find McCarthur's name at first, because it was partly smudged, and partly hidden. Then he found it and traced his finger in the air, trying to follow the labyrinth of hallways that led to the chamber. He looked to his left toward a doorway. Carina looked too and said, "No." She pointed to a different door several feet away, and they both nodded to each other.

10
Let Him Rot

The Boat Bar continued to ensure that the heartbeat of Key West would go on beating at a steady pace.

The heartbeat of Key West, of course, was illegal gambling at fixed tables for suckers who didn't know any better.

As always, Walter oversaw the racket, his hat slanted down over his eyes, his awareness taking in all activities across the establishment. The thin lanky man entered through the front door, and searched for Walter through the din and clatter.

He finally made out Walter's silhouette in his usual dark corner and started squeezing through the crowd toward him.

When he was close enough to be heard, he nodded at Walter and said matter-of-factly, "O'Doole put Trumbull on a boat and headed into the swamps. We were being followed."

"I know," Walter said.

"How'd you know?"

Walter lifted his head up so he could look the lanky man in the eye. He turned to his left and grabbed The Miami Herald. He tossed the paper at the lanky man and turned his gaze toward a poker table without saying anything.

The thin lanky man saw the headline for the first time. His hand began to shake slightly. He looked up at Walter. "What's our next move?"

Walter held his gaze toward the poker table. "We hope alligators eat Trumbull, O'Doole and Frankie, and hope they are never found or seen again."

The lanky man stood nervously. Walter finally turned to look at him. "You guys botched this one pretty good."

"What, uh – " the thin lanky man stopped, unsure what to say. "Are, are we going to go help out?"

"Is that what O'Doole sent you back here for?" Walter shook his head. "O'Doole's on his own. I never heard of him, and don't want to see him again. For tonight you can have his job, but it don't mean anything tomorrow."

11
Hack Reporter

Murphy led Carina through a dizzying sequence of hallways. He did not know for sure that they had taken all the right turns. Or any of the right turns, for that matter.

He stopped. He looked left, then right. Carina leaned forward from behind him, and peered down the hallway to the left.

Murphy took a step to his right and said, "I think it's down here."

Carina did not move after him. She kept her gaze to the left, concentrating intensely. Murphy stopped and turned back to her. "Carina?"

"It's this way," she said, moving confidently down the hallway to the left.

Murphy twisted his face into a wry smile and followed her.

They took two steps and froze.

A door opened at the end of the hallway. Belmont, Davis and Papy came through the door.

"You're a good man, McCarthur," Papy was saying, as he came forward through the door.

"Says you," McCarthur's voice rang out from inside the room, followed by a deep self-deprecating laugh.

The three men closed the door and patted each other on their respective backs.

"He's coming around," Davis said.

"He's one cagey fellow," said Belmont. "But in the end he knows what side his bread is buttered on."

"He's in our corner," Papy said. "He can't go to the mat yet, but he's in our corner."

Papy was confused by the awkward looks on the faces of Davis and Belmont. He followed their gazes, and found his confusion explained by the presence of Murphy and Carina at the end of the hallway facing them.

135

Murphy began walking toward the three men.

Papy made a motion as if he wanted to turn and run, but facing only McCarthur's door, he stopped, shook ever so slightly, and turned to face the oncoming Murphy and Carina.

Then Papy relaxed.

"Well," Papy said sunnily. "If it isn't Trumbull's little gopher."

"Morning Mr. Papy," Murphy began. "Would you care to comment on your recent presence in the judge's chamber?"

"What's the matter?" Papy asked. "Where's our dear Trumbull? Oh wait, I read it in the paper. So sad to hear. I do hope he comes through everything in one piece."

Murphy withdrew a small notepad from his jacket pocket and clicked a pen. "It's eight o'clock in the morning, Mr. Papy. I'll try one more time. What was the nature of your meeting just now in the private chamber of Judge McCarthur?"

Papy stepped forward and looked Murphy directly in the eye. "Libel and slander are serious offenses, kid," he said. "Especially from a hack reporter like you." Then he smiled and patted Murphy's cheek with the palm of his hand. "It's okay, though. I'm in a good mood. Write whatever you want, kid. You can't touch me."

He patted Murphy's cheek again, and half-turned to Davis and Belmont.

The three of them slid past Murphy and Carina and strode away down the hallway. They disappeared around the corner, and Murphy exhaled for the first time in several minutes.

Carina smiled at him and grabbed his arm, and they slowly walked back down the hallway in the direction they had come.

12
A Real Piece of Work

Trumbull slowly opened his eyes. A sharp pain shot through the left side of his neck. It was the pain of having slept awkwardly on the floor of a rowboat for the second night in a row. He lifted his head, only to smack it into O'Doole's shoe. O'Doole was also asleep, perched in a sitting position, his head drooped onto the forward bench seat of the rowboat. Frankie was wedged into the rear of the boat. His head hung out over the water. Mosquitoes swirled around Trumbull's head.

The boat drifted aimlessly along a dense mangrove shoreline.

Trumbull looked out over the edge of the boat. A tall thin great white heron perched itself on a mangrove root, poking its head into the water in search of food.

Trumbull sat up slowly. He looked toward the back of the boat at a crumpled bunch of waxed paper on the floor near Frankie's feet.

They had finished their meager supply of sandwiches the night before.

Trumbull was hungry. He swatted at the mosquitoes aimlessly. The mosquitoes laughed at him.

He reached into his coat pocket and pulled out his flask. He unscrewed the top.

Empty.

Trumbull took a deep breath and pulled himself up to a sitting position on the middle bench seat of the boat. He looked out at the wading bird. In the distance he heard an alligator grunt.

People survive out here all the time, he thought. There's plenty of food. It's just a matter of killing it and cooking it somehow.

Frankie stirred behind him.

Trumbull turned and looked at Frankie.

"Morning," Frankie said.

Trumbull nodded but didn't say anything.

Frankie stretched his stiff body. He exhaled, and looked around his feet at the empty waxed paper wrappings.

"Damn it," Frankie said.

Trumbull caught Frankie's eye and motioned his head toward the wading bird.

Frankie slowly turned from Trumbull to the bird.

"I don't know," Frankie said. "That's a little bit sickening."

"Suit yourself," Trumbull said.

"Now, alligator tail, that's a tasty dish," Frankie said.

"There's one nearby."

"All we got to do is shoot it," said Frankie.

"And then what?" Trumbull asked. "Eat it raw?"

"Well, I've heard that if you eat right away, it's good for you. Healthy. Before it has time to go bad."

Trumbull stared at Frankie for a moment. He nodded. "I'm game," he said. "Let's shoot a gator for breakfast."

"Got to wake up Rip Van Winkle over there."

Trumbull turned and looked at the still sleeping O'Doole. "He's afraid to let you carry your own gun?"

"No," Frankie said.

Trumbull remembered that Frankie had started the trip with his own gun. He did not remember what had happened to it. He looked quizzically at Frankie.

Frankie seemed embarrassed. Finally he admitted, "You were asleep. I threw it at a gator last night."

Trumbull smirked. "That's what I call grace under pressure. You threw your gun at a gator."

"I panicked," said Frankie.

"Never go to war," Trumbull said. "I'd hate to see what happens when you throw your rifle at a German."

The two of them sat in awkward silence. Frankie continued to eye O'Doole's hidden gun. He stood up slowly, trying not to rock the boat. Trumbull leaned to his left and Frankie took a step over his seat.

Frankie stood over the sleeping O'Doole. He reached delicately inside O'Doole's jacket, then grabbed the butt of the gun between his thumb and forefinger.

He began to pull the gun out.

O'Doole, suddenly alerted to the motion, awoke with a delirious howl, and reached blindly at the arm in front of him.

Frankie yelled at him while O'Doole yelled back, and a disoriented struggle, yelling match, and panic took place, climaxed by a thunderous bang, and then an ominous silence.

Then, O'Doole's voice began to moan.

"Oh, oh, god, oh god! Oh."

"Oh holy fuck," Frankie said quietly. Then more loudly, "O holy fuck!"

Trumbull dropped his head and muttered to himself, "I'm kidnapped by Laurel and Hardy....with guns."

He raised his head and looked at the scene at the front of the boat. O'Doole was clutching his shoulder and moaning. Blood was beginning to run down his shirt. Frankie was frozen, unable to make any sort of decision at all.

Giving in to the inevitability of the moment, Trumbull rose and moved toward O'Doole. He pushed Frankie out of the way and knelt down.

He grabbed O'Doole's hand and tried to move it away from the wound. O'Doole groaned and resisted Trumbull's attempt. Trumbull paused for a moment and tried again, this time more forcefully. He moved O'Doole's hand away and eyed the blood stain on O'Doole's shirt.

Slowly he unbuttoned the shirt and pulled it away from O'Doole's shoulder.

The entry wound was small. Blood oozed out and continued dripping down O'Doole's shoulder.

Trumbull tried to tear the shirt, but the fabric was too strong. He lowered his face to the blood-stained shirt and gripped the edge with his teeth. Pulling away with his teeth he ripped the shirt, then continued the tear with his hands, tossing the cleanly torn segment of fabric to the floor of the boat.

Trumbull turned back to the bloody shoulder. He placed his hand behind O'Doole's shoulder. O'Doole felt the force of his hand and groaned again. Trumbull pulled the shoulder forward. With a cry of pain O'Doole sat forward so Trumbull could see the back side of the shoulder.

Trumbull let O'Doole fall back against the edge of the boat.

He turned around from his kneeling position and looked at Frankie.

"No exit wound," Trumbull said. "We should get that bullet out. What tools you got?"

"Hm? Tools?" Frankie was still in a state of shock himself.

"Anything sharp? A knife? Nail file? Hell, you got any keys on you?"

Frankie reached into his pocket and pulled out a closed switch blade. He snapped the blade open and handed it to Trumbull. Trumbull took the blade, inspecting it carefully.

Trumbull reached over the edge of the boat and swished the blade in the swamp water. Then he took another close look at the blade and said, "Well, it's not sanitary, but any infection from this will be better than leaving the bullet in there."

Then Trumbull looked up at Frankie. "I'm going to need your help," he said.

"What do you want me to do?"

Trumbull paused for a moment and said, "When this goes in, O'Doole here is going to scream like a baby. I need you to hold him still. If he moves too much I'm going to cut him a lot more than I want to."

Frankie froze for a moment. "So... so you want me to –"

"I want you to hold him down," Trumbull said. "I want you to put a foot on his chest, and a hand on his other shoulder, like this." Trumbull showed him.

Frankie reluctantly raised his foot, and gently put it on O'Doole's chest.

Trumbull sighed. "Look," he said, "don't be afraid to use a little force. He has a bullet in him. Nothing you do with your foot is going to hurt him as much as that."

"Okay," Frankie nodded.

He put his foot on O'Doole's chest more forcefully, and propped his hand against O'Doole's right shoulder.

Trumbull reached down and gave the blade another swish through the swamp water, and raised it to his eye.

He took a breath, then touched the point of the blade to O'Doole's wound.

In a quick motion he cut the skin around the wound.

O'Doole cried out in a loud wail, and tried to move his shoulder.

"Hold him!" Trumbull shouted.

Frankie pushed down heavily to counteract O'Doole's writhing movement.

Trumbull quickly cut away some of the skin around the wound, and stuck his finger inside O'Doole's shoulder.

O'Doole screamed.

Trumbull quickly cut deeper with the blade, jamming it into the wound. He twisted once, twice, and wrenched the blade sideways.

He quickly stuck his finger into the wound and wedged the bullet to the surface of the wound. He pulled it out and dropped it to the floor of the boat.

In a quick motion Trumbull pushed Frankie away, and jumped into the swamp water. It was knee deep. He stood next to the boat, and grabbed O'Doole by the mid-section. With all his weight he pulled O'Doole out of the boat and into the water, nearly capsizing the boat in the process. Frankie dropped to his knees and held onto the rails of the boat to avoid falling in himself.

Trumbull submerged O'Doole's shoulder in the swamp water and washed the wound the best he could. Then he quickly lifted him up and yelled to Frankie, "Help me get him in, quick, before the gators find all this blood."

Together they lifted O'Doole back into the boat. Then Trumbull climbed in himself, and helped lay O'Doole out on the floor of the boat.

"Quick," Trumbull said, "let's get as far away from this blood as we can. Go, go."

Frankie grabbed the pole O'Doole had used earlier, and pushed at the floor of the swamp, edging the boat out through the trees, into an open area.

Trumbull kneeled down by O'Doole, and tore several pieces of his own shirt to strips. He used the strips to wrap O'Doole's wound the best he could.

Once they were safely away from the blood infested water, Trumbull looked up at Frankie and said, "So, first you throw your own gun at an alligator. Then you use his gun to shoot him in the shoulder. You're a piece of work, Frankie. You're a real piece of work."

Frankie did not respond. He continued pushing the boat out into the open water.

Trumbull looked back at the cluster of mangroves that had hidden them, then turned and looked out toward the open water.

The mosquitoes returned. A swarm hovered around the boat, defying Trumbull's and Frankie's frantic gesticulations.

Finally Trumbull gave up on the mosquitoes. He sat down and let them attack. Donating a little blood to a clan of mosquitoes was a better choice than fighting a losing battle.

"And still no breakfast," he said to no one in particular.

13
The Whole Truth

"Do we really even need Eva?" Belmont asked.

Papy, Davis, and Belmont were sitting across the coffee table from each other in the side room.

Belmont leaned back, exhaled heavily, and continued. "McCarthur has already ruled that matters outside of the purview of your buying votes in the state house are irrelevant. Eva, of course plays no role in the state house, so she might not be relevant to this case."

"I don't want to drop her from the list," said Papy. "I like her on the witness stand."

Davis cleared his throat. "I'm not the lawyer here," he said, "but I still think Eva can help us. She's agreed to give supportive testimony, and she, well, let's face it. She can sexy this trial up a little."

Belmont looked at Davis. "We're playing games," he said.

"That's fine by me as long as we win the games," Papy said.

"So," Belmont mused, "what do we gain from putting Eva on the witness stand?"

"We gain favorable exposure," Davis said.

"But she's a hooker."

"She's a madam," said Davis. "And she's not even that once she's on the witness stand. She's agreed to our story about being a dancer, a cultural ambassador. She's in charge of Key West's high minded arts interests."

"I don't know," Belmont mused.

Papy sat forward. "Put her on," he said. "I want to see something fun in the papers. Eva gives them a chance to sell papers, while she also paints a fine portrait of me."

"Can we trust her?" asked Belmont.

"She's squared away," Davis said. "She's not going to go off the script. She's been working on it."

"I don't know," Belmont continued. "I just worry. I mean, if she's not relevant, what's to be gained?"

"She's the best looking character witness I have," said Papy.

"We don't need character witnesses."

"Sure we do. Maybe not for the letter of the law. But we sure need character witnesses for the papers."

"The papers aren't going to decide the outcome of this case," Belmont said.

"That's for damn sure," said Papy.

A few minutes later everyone was settling back into their seats in courtroom B4.

Judge McCarthur adjusted the chair behind his bench and said loudly, "Back in session, blah blah blah. Let's get on with it. Where in the hell were we?"

Belmont stood and spoke with authority. "The defense would like to call to the witness stand Miss Eva Estevez."

All eyes turned as Eva, dressed elegantly, made her way down the aisle, through the small gate, and to the witness chair.

She hesitated before putting her hand on the bible in the bailiff's hand.

"Do you swear to tell the truth, the whole truth, and nothing but the truth, so help you God?"

"I do," Eva said, "but judging from some of the previous testimony, I assume it's not exactly a binding oath."

McCarthur bristled. "Just have a seat, miss," he said. "Any inappropriate sarcastic comments are my job in this courtroom."

As she sat, she swished her hair in a way that sent an audible lusty gasp through the courtroom.

She crossed her legs, showing all present a hint of thigh, smiled out at the room and nodded to Belmont.

"Miss Eva Estevez," Belmont began. "Would you care to relate to the court your professional relationship with the defendant, Representative Papy?"

Eva smiled at Belmont. "Of course. I am in charge of a house of prostitution in Key West, and pay kickbacks to Papy so he'll let me stay open."

The murmur from all present was deafening.

Papy was beyond angry.

Belmont turned to Papy and Davis and mouthed the words, "Now what?"

Davis did not respond. Instead he dropped his head into the fold of his arms.

Belmont quickly turned to McCarthur. "Your Honor, I request that this witness's testimony be stricken from the record, and her presence in this court be erased from all memory."

McCarthur chuckled. "Well, she's your witness, Belmont. What's wrong? She isn't testifying the way you coached her? Hells bells, what a tragedy."

"Your Honor – "

"And with all due respect," McCarthur continued, "We may all be dumb as stumps, but you can't erase our memory of her being on the witness stand. I mean look at her. You can't erase this."

Belmont stood silently for a moment. He searched his brain for a way out. He found none. He turned awkwardly back to Eva.

"Miss Estevez, is it not true that you are a patron and supporter of the arts in Key West?"

Eva smiled wryly. "I'm nothing of the kind. I run a prostitution business. Why, I think I've even seen your face there. You spent a nice big chunk of cash to roll in the hay with Charlene, enjoyed it too, as I recall. Told Charlene you were in love with her."

Belmont coughed and turned to Papy and Davis. Davis made a quick slicing motion under his throat, and Belmont turned back to Eva. "Okay, Miss Estevez. You can step down now."

"Excuse me," one of the well-dressed lawyers at the prosecution table shouted. "The witness has not been cross examined."

"Your Honor," Belmont grunted desperately.

McCarthur laughed openly. "The witness may be cross-examined by the prosecution."

Belmont was defeated. "Objection, Your Honor," he said weakly.

"Objection noted," said McCarthur. "Overruled."

"Exception," Belmont coughed.

"Noted," said McCarthur. "Mr. Belmont, you can sit down now. All your objections and exceptions, and what not, are recorded. There ain't nothing left for you to say. You walked into a pile of horse manure, and now you're just gonna have to wade around in it. Prosecution's witness."

The well dressed lawyer suppressed a faint smile as he stood. He paused before walking around the corner of the table and approaching Eva.

"Miss Estevez," he began, "I wonder if the court was allowed a full and complete picture of the exact nature of your – " he coughed for effect, then continued, "uh, your professional relationship with Representative Papy."

"I pay him," Eva said. "I take a percentage of my profits and hand them over to Papy, and in exchange, as long as he's making money from it himself, he leaves me alone to run the business."

"And how long has this arrangement been in place?"

Well," Eva mused, "I guess if you go back to when Thelma ran the place before me, about fifteen years now."

The lawyer turned toward the defendant's table. "Miss Estevez, are there any other details you would like to share with the court?"

"Oh, just little tidbits, like the fact that Papy hands out money during election campaigns, buys votes to keep getting re-elected. You know, the usual." Eva sat back in the witness chair.

The lawyer turned back to her and thought for a moment. "Miss Estevez, does your current testimony divert from the testimony you were coached to give here this afternoon?"

"Yes. I was coached to lie. I decided to tell the truth. Call me corny. I respect that little oath I took before sitting down."

The lawyer was silent for another moment, then raised his head to look at Eva. "What consequences do you expect after testifying in this manner?"

Eva took a breath before answering. "Well, one time they burned down the building where I used to run the business. They've shut me down, slapped my girls around. I expect I'll be put out of business for good now."

"And yet, knowing that you were in danger of being put out of business, you insisted on telling us all these provocative details."

"Maybe I've spent too much time with Mr. Trumbull. He's a journalist. He likes the truth. Some of that has rubbed off on me."

"Thank you Miss Estevez. No further questions."

The buzz in the court room was palpable.

Eva stood and began her exit. As she passed through the aisle she made eye contact with Pat Murphy. He nodded to her.

She did not respond. She just kept walking.

Sitting next to Murphy, Carina caught the moment and felt the slightest twinge of jealousy.

14
Release from Captivity

The boat drifted lazily from the coastline of the Everglades, out across the shallow water of Florida Bay.

Frankie sat at the rear of the boat, hunched over, holding his stomach, staring down blankly at the floor of the boat.

Trumbull was hungry, and showed it. The stubble of his beard gave him the look of a combat soldier who was hunkered down in a fox hole for a couple days too many. Unlike Frankie though, he kept his gaze on the horizon, searching for any sign of a rescue boat.

O'Doole lay on the floor of the boat, unconscious but alive.

Together, the three men looked like a trio you wouldn't want anything to do with.

Time passed without acknowledgment.

The boat drifted further. No one guided it. It just drifted.

Then Trumbull heard something behind him. It was just the slightest sound, but sometimes lack of food sharpens a person's senses.

He turned back to the coastline of the Everglades.

There, a good mile and a half away, drifting out from the cover of trees and swamp grass, were two boats.

In the distance, Trumbull could faintly make out the excited back and forth of voices.

He waited. The two boats seemed to be coming in his direction. All he really cared about was that they might have sandwiches.

It took a while, but eventually the two boats were close enough to shout to. Trumbull didn't shout, though. He sat calmly, watching them approach. Finally Frankie turned and followed Trumbull's gaze.

Frankie looked back at Trumbull and dropped his head.

He recognized the FBI when he saw them.

148

Then the voice echoed across the several remaining yards of open bay, "Are you Stephen Trumbull?"

Trumbull raised his head and looked at the boat tiredly. "Not for much longer, unless you have some food."

"We're the FBI. Are you alright?"

"I'm alright," Trumbull shouted back. "But we have a guy here who needs a hospital pretty bad."

Moments later the two FBI boats pulled up on opposite sides of the drifting row boat. Trumbull stood and stepped over the railing into the larger of the two FBI boats. Two men jumped into the row boat and knelt down over O'Doole.

"He's breathing," one of them yelled.

They carefully moved O'Doole into one of the FBI boats, and then handcuffed Frankie. They tied the small boat behind the larger FBI boat, and got to work making their way back to civilization.

At The Miami Herald, Hills sat in his office and took the good news over the phone. He was relieved to call in one of his staff reporters to write the story.

"Don't make a big deal about it being Trumbull," Hills told the reporter. "Just write the facts. He was kidnapped, and he made it through okay. The FBI found him and his captors. They have released him. Nothing flowery."

"Got it," the reporter said.

Then Hills tried to call Murphy with the good news, but failed to find him at the hotel.

15
The Saint

One by one, Papy's compromised colleagues made their way to the witness stand to recount what a loving, generous, selfless saint of a man Representative Bernie Papy was.

They painted a picture of a giving man, a man who cared for friends like they were family.

On cross examination their stories seemed to take on a slightly more sinister hue.

One minute a colleague from the state legislature was singing Papy's praises as a man who helped pass a bill to help underprivileged children. On cross examination it turned out that a deal was forced on the gentleman, under duress, in exchange for his support of a power grab by Papy. Along with the threats always came a healthy dose of gift giving.

Murphy took meticulous notes. Papy knew his stuff. A portrait took shape. Papy always balanced threats with gifts. He would scare you one moment, help you out of a jam the next, demand your loyalty, demand your money, and then give you something you held dear and valuable to round out the bargain.

And finally it was Papy's turn to tell his own story.

Belmont stood confidently at the defendant's table.

McCarthur looked out over his reading glasses. "Everybody hold onto your hats," McCarthur said. "The big song and dance number is about to hit the stage."

"Your Honor," Belmont said loudly, "The defense would like to call to the witness stand, Florida State Representative Bernie Papy."

"I'm sure you would," McCarthur responded. "Well, I guess there's nothing I can do to prevent it. Get on with yourself."

Papy stood next to Belmont. He brushed his jacket with his hands and turned to walk to the witness stand.

"Do you swear to tell the truth, the whole truth, and nothing but the truth, so help you God?"

"I do," said Papy, and he sat in the chair with an air of mastery.

Belmont stepped around the corner of the defendant's table, and approached Papy silently.

Three rows back, surrounded by other reporters, Murphy began to feel sick. Carina, sitting next to him, turned toward Murphy. He was pale. He slowly handed his notebook to Carina. "Take notes," he whispered, and got up to leave.

Papy noticed Murphy leaving and twisted his expression.

Outside in the hallway Murphy walked quickly, holding his stomach.

He pushed open the door to the bathroom, and rushed to a stall. Then he felt fine. As quickly as it had started the feeling passed.

He stood, turned to a mirror, brushed his hair with his hand and took a couple of deep breaths.

He walked back out into the hallway. The hallway was deserted. Everyone was in the courtroom listening to Papy spin his feel-good magic.

Murphy approached the door to the court room. He could hear Papy on the witness stand. Then the feeling returned. Murphy held his stomach and suppressed the need to vomit. Then he realized what had hit him.

It wasn't illness. It wasn't an upset stomach.

Murphy realized at that moment that he had lost his tolerance for double-speak. He could no longer listen to a politician spin the truth into something it wasn't. It made him physically ill.

Later, when he would eventually tell Trumbull, Trumbull would tell him this was the moment when he actually became a reporter.

He went back to the bathroom, turned on the water in the sink, and cupped his hand. He slurped several mouthfuls of water. It was cold, and felt good going down.

He straightened up, wiped the leftover water from his face, and went back out into the hallway.

This time he went back into the courtroom, squeezed his way back into his seat, took the notebook back from Carina, and finally listened to Papy's testimony, or what was left of it. He looked Papy directly in the eye, felt disdain, and wrote something in the notebook.

Papy paused for a split second as Murphy looked at him.

"Representative Papy?" Belmont said, questioningly.

"I'm sorry, um, what was I saying?"

"Can the court clerk read back the testimony where Mr. Papy left off?"

The clerk checked the paper. "I love my people. I love them too much. Maybe that's why I sometimes get into a little trouble trying to do what's right for them."

"Ah, yes, of course," Papy said. "That's all then. That was the end of the sentence."

"Your witness," Belmont said, turning to the prosecution table.

The well dressed lawyer stood slowly, going over last minute notes. He stepped away from his chair and approached Papy.

"Representative Papy," the lawyer began, "how do you respond to the allegations of Representative Traynor?"

"You'll forgive me," said Papy, "but I don't remember what Mr. Traynor has alleged."

"Put simply, Mr. Papy, Representative Traynor has accused you of placing a one-hundred dollar bill in his hand while you shook said hand."

"Ah, that," Papy said, smiling.

He looked down as if recalling a fond memory. Several seconds passed in silence.

"Representative Papy?" the lawyer prodded.

Papy looked up. He took a breath and looked out at the courtroom. "Yes," he said proudly, "I will admit I did try to give Traynor a one-hundred dollar bill."

A buzz erupted from the crowd.

"Order! Order!" McCarthur commanded. "Come on, now. Everyone keep your drawers dry."

All eyes were on Papy as he prepared to elaborate.

"Sir," he said, looking up at the lawyer, "do you have any children?"

"I do not sir, but that is beside the point."

"I do," Papy said. "I am the proud father of Bernie Papy, Jr. My pride and joy. He has graduated recently. I gave him a cash gift as a graduation present. Were there strings attached? Absolutely not. I was delighted to give him a gift. I am a giving person."

The lawyer stood for a moment before responding. "Are we to gather, from this story, Mr. Papy, that you were somehow treating Representative Traynor as a son of yours?"

"I was trying to welcome a newly elected public servant to the state assembly. I was trying to make him feel welcome and wanted. Imagine my disappointment when he rejected my gift and somehow twisted it into a scandal."

The crowd was holding their breath. Murphy was feeling sicker than he had before. He felt a sudden impulse to run up to the witness stand and vomit directly on Representative Papy.

"And as to Traynor's pending bill to regulate bookies?" the lawyer asked. "Had you not just completed a hard-fought legislative battle to kill a similar bill?"

"That's neither here nor there," Papy said.

"Mr. Papy, I can assure you that it was indeed 'here and there.'"

"I was being generous," Papy continued. "I asked for nothing in return for my gift. I simply wanted a novice legislator to feel welcome."

It was too much for Murphy. He threw the notebook back in Carina's lap, bolted from the courtroom, ran down the hallway, and barely made it before the contents of his stomach found their way into the nearest toilet bowl.

He was more angry than sick, though.

Alone in the bathroom, Murphy weakly punched the metal stall door. He punched it over and over again, until the knuckles of his hand began to swell.

Finally, he sat back against the stall door, looking up dejectedly at the ceiling.

He breathed heavily. He looked at his swollen knuckles, turning his hand over and over. He gave the metal stall divider one last punch and dropped his head back with a heavy sigh.

16
The Last Reunion?

Eva sat in her hotel room, staring out the window dejectedly.

The knock on her hotel room door sounded familiar. She looked toward the door, wondering if it could be him. She knew it was.

"Come on in, Trumbull," she called out.

Trumbull opened the door and came in from the hallway.

"How'd you know it was me?"

"Nobody knocks like you," she said.

Trumbull closed the door and tossed his hat on the bed. He walked toward her. She didn't get up.

"I heard you were quite a hit in court," Trumbull said.

"Yeah? I heard you were kidnapped and rescued by the FBI."

"I guess we both have interesting stories."

She looked up at him. Her expression did not show as much emotion as he had expected. He sat in the chair facing her.

"You're welcome," she said.

"For what? For giving my home address to Walter and Cranston?"

"For putting the FBI on your tail," she said.

Trumbull looked down and thought for a moment. "Yes, I suppose I should thank you for that."

"Now who do I thank for being put out of business?"

Trumbull followed her gaze out the window. "Well, you'll have to thank Papy himself for that."

"I almost moved back to Havana last time," Eva said. "Maybe now I'll have to." She turned to Trumbull. "Unless you have any place I can stay."

"I tried that with someone," Trumbull said. "I decided I have to live alone."

"You're no gentleman, Trumbull."

"Since when did I ever try to be?"

"I was just stating the obvious."

Trumbull looked at her with a mix of annoyance and appreciation. He reached out and put his hand on her cheek. He rubbed her skin gently.

"You know, Eva, I'm impressed with you. I'm more impressed as time goes by. You're the best."

She didn't respond. She looked down at the floor.

Trumbull removed his hand and sat back in the chair.

After a minute of silence Trumbull stood up. "Well, he said, so much for fireworks. I guess I'll be going."

Eva looked up quickly, and stood to face him.

She raised her arm and hooked her elbow around his neck and pulled him into a kiss before he realized it was happening.

He kissed her back, and for a brief moment there was nothing else, no trial, no newspaper, no lost business.

She pulled out of the kiss. Their eyes were close.

"Was that good bye?" he asked.

"I don't know," she said.

"For a minute there I was thinking maybe you didn't like me anymore."

"Yeah," she said, smiling. "I was thinking that too."

17
Not Guilty

The boys who shout the front page headlines from the street corner like big bold headlines more than subtle nuanced headlines.

"Papy found not guilty!" has the kind of splash to it that a paper boy can throw his weight into.

The story, as Murphy wrote it, had subtlety to it. It had nuance. But the headline spoke for itself.

As Murphy wrote it, Judge Ian McCarthur had a field day wrapping up the prosecution's failings.

"Hell," the story quoted McCarthur as saying, "I even agree with you guys. Papy is as rotten as a month-old turtle carcass. You boys utterly failed to prove the specifics of this case. Is Papy a crooked, corrupt, back-room dealing, double-speaking jackass? Hell yes. But that's not what he was on trial for here. This trial was set up to prove one thing and one thing only; did he buy votes in the state assembly? And I've never seen a more comical failure to prove a guilty man guilty. Why, I even planned to give Papy some sort of pointless token slap on the wrist, but I can't even do that. Papy is free to go."

Murphy also reported that the prosecution immediately filed for a mistrial based on the inappropriate private meetings between Papy and McCarthur.

For Papy the table was set perfectly.

The microphone was set up on the steps of the Florida State Capital building. The waiting crowd of reporters had broken into separate groups, chatting with each other.

Murphy and Carina looked comfortable together as Trumbull approached.

"Look who's back from taming alligators," Murphy said.

Trumbull nodded to Murphy and replied, "Alligators refuse to be tamed."

157

"You call Hills yet?" Murphy asked. "He's been acting like a worried mother hen."

"No, not yet. I'll call him."

Carina asked, "Have you eaten, Trumbull? I heard you went hungry for a while."

"Yes, I'm fine."

Then they were interrupted by the arrival of the man of the hour.

Papy emerged from the capital building doorway, Davis at his side, and walked confidently down the stairs towards the microphone.

The buzz of the reporters conversations quieted.

"Hello, good morning," Papy said. "Thank you for coming. I will make this brief." He cleared his throat and scanned the crowd quickly. His eyes met Trumbull's. Trumbull looked at him coldly. Papy shook slightly, then took a breath and continued.

"Once again the witch hunt has failed," he said. "The great justice system of these United States has exonerated me from false accusations and slanderous lies. Thankfully, I am free to attend to the needs of my people, the great citizens of Monroe County. I can only hope and trust that the lies and the innuendos will now be put to bed for good. Thank you."

Then he turned away quickly and walked up the steps, ignoring the barrage of questions from the gathered reporters.

Trumbull did not yell any questions toward the retreating Papy. What's the point, he thought. He looked at Murphy. Carina put a pen away and closed the notebook she was writing in.

"Let's get out of here," Trumbull said.

"Yes," Murphy agreed. "Let's go. We've got to get back to the Key West bureau and dig up some new innuendos to write about this guy."

"He wants the slander to stop," Trumbull mused. "Unfortunately, for him, the truth will continue."

18
Still Here

Dear Cuz;

I'm still here. I shouldn't be.

Papy scheduled my disappearance. Unfortunately for him, Abbot and Costello showed up to carry out his plan. Not only did they fail to rub me out, they nearly caused their own demise. Comedy, more than respect, seems to follow Papy around.

Papy has a good set up. He puts on a soft shoe song and dance and the public eats it up.

I know better though.

The most dangerous mistake a reporter can make, though, is to assume that just because you report the truth, the reader will, in turn, actually care.

Don't get me wrong, I know many of you dear readers do care. I get too many letters from you. I know you care.

There just doesn't seem to be enough of you.

Papy keeps getting re-elected. Year after year, session after session, he trots out his song and dance, hands out a little cash to his voters, pats everyone on the back. Then he threatens and intimidates anyone who would stand up to him, and presto! Business as usual.

So Papy is still standing. And so am I.

What is business as usual for Papy? Just to review; he runs Key West. Gambling – though it remains illegal – is his life blood. Your misguided attempt to win a little free cash from his town, from his ramshackle casinos, funds a wide array of corrupt investments.

And business as usual for me?

I will dog Papy as long as I can draw a breath.

I understand that in reporting the truth it does not necessarily follow that you will care.

I can do nothing else, though. The stakes demand it.

-Trumbull

Peter Wick's films

Rock Paper Scissors won Wick the Best Director Award at the New York International Film Festival in 2011. It tells the story of Marty (Wick), the ex-basketball star turned PE teacher, and Lana, his long ago high school sweetheart, now the eccentric high school science teacher (former "Miss Italy" Roberta Orlandi). When they meet, years after their original affair, old passions re-ignite. But she's married, he's not. Romance, passion, and humor combine to tell a very human story.

Available on Amazon

Movie Pizza Love won the Indiefest's Feature Film Award-of-merit in 2008, as well the Original Song award for co-star Jen Casebeer's song, "Trashy Novel." The ultimate low budget film, Wick made this award-winning feature with a total budget of just $5,000, shooting over three weeks with a volunteer crew. "Art" (Wick) is making a film about his singer-songwriter friend Lisa (Casebeer). The movie-within-a-movie (within-a-movie) twists in on itself, as Art slowly realizes the friend is more important than the movie. Funny, thoughtful, and unpredictable, this film has been included on more than 100 'favorite films' lists around the world.

Available on Amazon

Long Strange Trip, Wick's debut feature, won him the "Most Promising Director" award at 1999's NYIIFVF. The film follows "Phil" (Wick) on a bizarre, twisted descent into absurdity, billed as a 'comic homage' to "Apocalypse Now." After losing his magazine column, his book deal, and his relationship with his Editor/girlfriend Andrea, Phil is assigned to interview a stripper. When the stripper's brother Lars enters the story, sporting a festering bullet wound to the head, all sanity is lost. Included on several lists of longest movie titles of all time, the full title of the film is, "Long Strange Trip – or The Writer, The Naked Girl, and The Guy with a hole in his Head."
Available at Indieflix.com

www.peter-wick.com

Twitter: @juventinopw
Blog: www.peterwick.blogspot.com
Youtube: Azzurri Productions

Peter Wick's books

Key West – Special Edition (2015) combines Wick's original 2013 novel with prequel short story, "The King of the Keys." Inspired by real events, ***Key West*** chronicles the 1950's battle between corrupt Florida state representative Bernie Papy, and 'hardboiled' journalist, Miami Herald columnist Stephen Trumbull. Mark Howell of the Key West Citizen called Wick's novel, "An engaging, fun read," and one Amazon customer review raved "[I] cannot put it down."

Key West – The Companion Episodes (2015) brings Wick's original 2013 and 2014 follow-up episodes (originally published by Wheelman Press as kindle-only novellas) together under one cover for the first time. It is 1951 and Florida state representative Bernie Papy is pulling all the strings. Trumbull is using his Miami Herald column to expose Papy. "The Companion Episodes" tells a gripping story of danger, corruption, backroom deals, and Trumbull's relentless search for the truth.

It Is What It Is (Summer 2015) Seventeen years ago Zenny Zeller was the drummer of one-hit wonder band "Gupper Fish." Now he rents space in his house to the beautiful Stella and her band. Stella's drummer, I.Q., has disappeared….again. Zenny and the band bumble through one possible lead after another, hoping to find I.Q. before their big club show for industry mogul, Glazer-from-Polymorph. Along the way they encounter an endless parade of colorful characters, some of them burned out old friends of Zenny's from "back in the day." This new light hearted novella from Wick humorously weaves a fun and funny tale, inspired in part by Wick's own history on the fringes of the "grunge" music scene.